Mark McKnight was born in Lisburn, Northern Ireland. He is an author, a teacher, a musician, a film maker and a missionary in that order. Hopefully, this arrangement will change in the not too distant future. He currently lives in Northallerton, North Yorkshire (England) but in his own words, "It's not Ireland and it's not Africa!" He has also told and written a plethora of other short and longer stories (many of which are longer than 500 words), the first published collection of which is *Msimulizi: Stories for Mwangaza*. This is soon to be succeeded by two sequels – *Msimulizi 2: The Green Dragon* and another as yet untitled work, no doubt beginning with the words, '*Msimulizi 3...*'

500 is his second printed work.

♠◇♣♡

Forthcoming and already available titles
by Mark McKnight

Msimulizi: Stories For Mwangaza
Msimulizi 2: The Green Dragon

The Village At The End Of The World

On The Road

For more copies of this book, for other titles (including CDs and
DVDs), information and contact details, please visit

http://www.babymosquito.com

At the time of press, Mark McKnight is affiliated with Africa Renewal
Ministries and the Mwangaza Children's Choir. All proceeds from this
book will go towards Mark's continuing ministry as a missionary to the
children of Uganda, East Africa.

♠ ◇ ♣ ♡

500

♠ ◇ ♣ ♡

A Collection Of Very Short Stories

By Mark McKnight

Baby Mosquito Books

Acknowledgements

My most heartfelt gratitude is for Almighty God for pulling me out of that car wreck. Thank God 'On A Stormy Tuesday Afternoon' is just a story.

Then in no particular order, thanks are also due to Adam Ansel, Barry and Vicky Thompson, my family, Mwai, Sabina, Elsa, Ivan and all the children who went to Mombassa with us, the village of Gaba for their continuing inspiration, the girl who was almost the girl in the pink dress and everyone in my life who has been an encouragement to my creativity, a stimulus for a story or a muse for my creative spirit.

Copyright © 2005 by Mark McKnight

First published in 2006 by Baby Mosquito Books

The right of Mark McKnight to be identified as the Author of the Work has been asserted by him in accordance with the Copyright, Designs and Patents Act 1988.

ISBN 1-905691-01-7
ISBN 978-1-905691-01-2

This book has been typeset in Times New Roman, Arial, Playing Cards, Justice, Bermuda Solid and Cards

Printed and bound in Great Britain by Lightning Source Inc, Milton Keynes

Mark McKnight
87 Killowen Grange
Lisburn
Co. Antrim
BT28 3JE
NORTHERN IRELAND

http://www.babymosquito.com
mark@babymosquito.com

For Pete

A solemn promise is almost fulfilled in the first part. We shall soon be compelled to make good our pact for the second part. Although we have many times been silent, our prayers have been ever with you. But you have passed through the flames and have emerged a better man. More complete than before. It is time.

And For Adam

A book for a book.
A lifetime of stories to tell.
A friend, a brother, an adventurer, a co-conspirator and an inspiration.

Contents

♠◇♣♡

500

♠◇♣♡

Prologue

The number 500 is singular in a variety of ways. It is a Harshad number (which means nothing to me but apparently it's something impressive). In Roman numerals, it is written 'D.' In binary, '111110100' and in hexadecimal '1F4.' 500 years ago was the middle of the French Revolution. It is an HTTP status code denoting and Internal Server Error and an SMTP status code denoting a syntax error due to an unrecognised command. It is well known in context as the Indianapolis 500 and the Fortune 500. 500 (the card game) is the national card game of Australia and it is also the model number of a popular car by Ford. It is a game that can be played with a Frisbee or a ball, getting its name by the number of points you need to win.

To begin with, 500 (the book) was something of an experiment. An experiment in succinct story telling. A question as to whether or not the brevity of five hundred words would be enough to fully tell a story. As time went on, the idea snowballed into a book of stories, each with five hundred words exactly. The following is the result of my experiment. Each of the fifty three stories in this book has exactly 500 words – no more, no less which means (not including this preamble) there are exactly 26,500 words of story telling to be read.

The very first 500 word story was written during a lecture at Durham University on 23rd October, 2004. One on a very bumpy bus ride between Mombassa and Nairobi in August, 2005 and another at Ennyumba ye Kitangaala (House of Light) in Gaba, Uganda. The rest were written in Brompton, Brompton on Swale and at Applegarth Primary School – all in the environs of Northallerton, North Yorkshire, the area where I currently find myself residing. The last story was written on 14th November, 2005.

The order of the stories is not as arbitrary as it may seem. Actually, the order of the stories is completely arbitrary. Each story was assigned to a card in a deck (including one joker). The deck was then shuffled seven times (using a Vegas shuffle rather than the Reno shuffle favoured by Bryn when he whipped our lily white butts at poker). Apparently, seven is the optimal number to mix a deck properly. The order of the deck is the order of the stories that you will see in the following pages.

These stories are something of a departure from my previous book (Msimulizi: Stories for Mwangaza). Adam was a little shocked when I emailed him the first 500 word story: many of these stories are not suitable for children. You may ask how a Christian and a missionary can write stories like this? My only answer is that a story chooses the teller rather than the other way around. I have written about things I am passionate about – events in my life, places I have visited and friends I have known. I have also written many stories of pure fiction – things that I thought would make a good tale. In Ireland, they say that I like to spin a good yarn.

If you recognise yourself in the stories or you know the events or places that inspired them, don't be flattered or offended. Please remember that this is only intended to be fiction. Some of them are based on actual things: only the names, places and events have been changed!

Even though a story is written in the first person, please don't think that it represents my own opinions. In many of my stories, I have tried to put myself in the position of someone else and tell their tale. In some, I have written about how I felt at a different time in a different period in my life. In others, the main character deliberately appears narrow minded, foolish, conceited or vain.

I love to write. When I wake in the morning, it's the first thing I think of. Maybe God will bless me in the future and give me a writing contract but while I'm still an amateur, please enjoy my stories. If you like them, please tell me. If you don't, tell me how I can make them better.

I some cases, I have succeeded in saying all that needs to be said in just five hundred words. In others, I may not have accomplished my task. I will leave you to be the judge…

And if you're reading and your name is Kay McKnight or Vicki Hardman, none of the stuff in these stories ever really happened…Honest!

Stolen Roses

By Mark McKnight

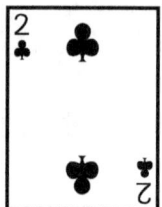

I did something rather foolhardy today. Despite what my wife believes, I have in fact been working late for the last couple of months. That's not a euphemism either, believe me.

This evening, I managed to finish work only an hour after I should have, jumped into my car and was looking forward to a quiet night in front of the fire with my wife of 18 years. So I stopped for petrol on the way home. After I had paid, some flowers caught my eye and, since it had been a while, I thought I would buy my wife some roses. A dozen red roses to be precise.

Unfortunately, as I picked up my roses, my mobile phone rang – it was work with another 'emergency.' As a middle manager with visions of greatness, when work says 'Jump', I say, 'How high?' So I threw the roses in the back seat and sped back to my place of employment. This action turned my bunch of roses into a bunch of stolen roses.

One of our more lucrative clients was having a problem with an insurance claim and, I was assured, this was the only time she could set aside to talk about it. As I entered the boardroom, I winced as her perfume assaulted my nasal passages. It wasn't that it smelled bad per se. Just that she was wearing so much of it.

As loss adjuster of the month for eight months running, I was the natural choice to deal with this kind of emergency and so everything was done and dusted within the hour, now making me two hours late to return to my wife.

As I fumbled in the outside pockets of my jacket for my car keys, I found the receipt for my petrol. It was only then that I remembered about the flora currently residing in the rear seat of my automobile – I hadn't paid for them. I sped back to the petrol station to try to make amends but by now they were closed for the night. In

♠◇♣♡

retrospect, leaving them on the doorstep of a petrol station forecourt with a note saying sorry was rather imprudent but I was weary and not entirely in my right mind. Had I known the consequences of my actions, I would certainly not have been so reckless.

Returning to my home, my castle, I found my beloved like a tiger ready for the kill. The look on her face hinted at the approaching storm. It seems that my crime had been captured in glorious Technicolor on CCTV. The police had tracked me down from my number plate and had visited, mentioning to my wife the nature of my crime.

I knew circumstances were dire when my wife greeted me with the line, "Those flowers better be for me..." The flowers that I had left at the petrol station. When she smelled the perfume, it was all over.

It's hard to get comfortable on two-seater sofa, you know!

26.10.05
Brompton, England

♠◇♣♡

A Pound For The Bus

By Mark McKnight

It wasn't so much that I had a big no drugs policy. I didn't have a T-shirt or posters or anything like that. I had heard all the drugs talks. SAY NO TO DRUGS. It was more that I'd never really had the opportunity to try them. Maybe I moved in the wrong circles of friends. Maybe I had a sheltered upbringing although in Lisburn, I'm not sure how I could have.

So that is why at the age of nineteen, I had never really done any drugs. Of course I smoked for a bit when I was a teenager but that was it as far as my drug habit went.

As I ambled along my street one day without anything in particular to do, I met 'Cider Man' as he came to be known for his habit of drinking cider outside our house. He opened with, "Could you spare me a pound for the bus to get home." My belief was that my pound would not go towards a bus fare but rather a two litre bottle of Strongbow or other such fermented apple beverage as would (as the rhyme alludes) make him happy and possibly cause a certain jovial flatulence.

But this conversation took an unexpected turn when he, without warning, abandoned his original line of questioning in favour of a discussion of what we may call 'non-prescribed medication' or more specifically pot. It seemed he was in fact a pot-head and the whole cider thing was just a red herring.

He even had an offer for me, a chance to supplement my paltry student loan with an extra income. It seemed he was something of a local celebrity. This made it very difficult for him to conduct his business – that of distributing his pot to the masses. Pot which, I am reliably informed, was 'first class shit, man, freaking mind melting.' His offer was for me to act as a middle man in the pubs and clubs, on the highways and byways.

♠◇♣♡

I could obviously build in my own profit margins. I would be paid on commission but would have to pay for stock up front. Tax was optional as this was a 'contra-legal' enterprise. However, I would be expected to make voluntary National Insurance contributions as this was expected of most people not on benefits.

He did not explain this in so many words. What he actually said was, "You can make a f**king fortune at this man," but I was able to infer the rest from his tone of voice and demeanour. As for the fortune, I remain unconvinced. He seems to be a poor case in point for his line of business.

So I made my excuses and hastened my departure. I did give him a pound for the bus in the vain hope that he would remove his cider/pot induced alternate reality to outside someone else's house. No such luck. He returned in less than an hour with a new bottle of cider.

31.10.05
Brompton, England

10p Toilet

By Mark McKnight

As I walked home the other night, I came upon a public lavatory. Feeling nature's call, I decided this was an opportune moment to spend a penny. Gone are the days when one spent a mere penny. On this particular evening, I was scandalised to the tune of ten English pennies to use this public convenience. Of course, one must pay a high price for such premium services as the self cleaning W.C.

I have always had an aversion to public toilets. After all, what if someone were to hear me in my ablutions? No other embarrassment could compare.

My trip to this particular water closet began as a fairly mundane experience. Until, that is, I flushed the cistern twice in quick succession and the wall revolved to reveal a gateway to a parallel dimension. "Hmmm…" thought I. As this was a somewhat odd venue for this important disruption to the space time continuum, I decided to investigate further. In retrospect, my actions were foolish but we often look back on the past with rose tinted spectacles.

No out of body experience or alien abduction seemed imminent so I passed through the worm hole with a minimum of fuss. After all, we English are renowned for our unflappable calm under pressure. The stiff upper lip so to speak.

Imagine my surprise when I was met on the other side of the trapdoor to an alternate reality by a most beautiful alien life form – flowing locks and dressed to kill. This alien being greeted me in a strange dialect and offered me refreshments. Not wanting to appear rude and to put my host at ease, I gratefully accepted her offer of sustenance and promptly settled down for my much needed rest.

However, it became apparent that sleep was not to be forthcoming that night. Entertainment had been laid on – fire dancers, sword jugglers and singers of strange songs were paraded in front of me until well into the 'wee small hours.' I thought about venturing my plan to spend some few hours sleeping but I feared it would cause offence to my hosts and thus remained silent, applauding at the appropriate moments.

Finally, I was allowed to sleep, in a communal bedroom along with a two and a half ton elephant. Interestingly, the aliens seemed to ignore the elephant – moving around it as if it were not there. This struck me as somewhat odd since nobody seemed to talk about this elephant in the room. However, I did not want to seem naïve or rude so I once again remained silent and did not mention the elephant in the room, despite the fact that it took up more than half of the available space.

The following morning, I was led back through the portal to my own world to return to my own life. As I repaired to the toilet cubicle from whence I came, my mind was filled with confusion and thoughts. From my mouth uttered the single syllable, "Hmmm…"

30.9.05
Northallerton, England

In The Heat Of Passion

By Mark McKnight

A man may do strange things in the heat of passion. The relationship between a man and a wife is a sacred thing: what God has joined together, let no man put asunder. Of course, this stance presents a quandary for the would-be infidel (one given to the practices associated with infidelity). It is not right that a woman should put up with an unfaithful husband. It seems even more unfair for a man have to suffer the injustices of this life laid upon him by an adulterous wife. What is a man to do with an unfaithful wife? I repeat, a man may do strange things in the heat of passion. By nature, a wife is something worth fighting for. Otherwise, marriage is a well packaged scam – a tax on fools. But it would be myopic to think that every marriage is a happy one.

A certain man returned to his home, his castle to find his wife in the process of gaining carnal knowledge of a man he knew to be someone other than her husband for he himself was currently filling that position. In the same bed in which his own marriage had been consummated, this Jezebel was betraying him with another man. This certain man had several advantages over the wife and her gigolo: the element of surprise, a state of fully clothedness and adrenaline coursing through his veins. On the other hand, the red mist had descended and he did not have the benefit of coherent thought or regard for the law of the land.

Entering his bedroom with a rope, he deftly tied his wife and her lover together– whatever happened from here on in was for both of them. Time spent in the scouts as a lad had finally come in handy – these knots were inescapable. That is where his plan ended and he paused to decide what to do with them next.

They were led naked to the garden where they were tied to the apple tree that this man had carefully planted on the day they were

♠◇♣♡

married as a symbol of their love. As the wife and her fancy man begged for mercy, the man showed none. How could he have any feeling towards anyone who would do something like this? They were gagged so that they would not attract attention or scream for help and left as the man returned indoors. As he entered, he felt no warmth from his own house – his wife had removed all the warmth from his soul. There was now only coldness.

During the bitterly cold night, hypothermia set in to the wife and her toy boy and in the early hours of the morning, they both succumbed to the sub zero temperatures and died where they stood – tied to the tree.

The next morning, reality began to set in. The man looked through the dirty glass of the kitchen window and saw the awkwardly slumped bodies against the apple tree. Instantly, he knew.

7.11.05
Brompton, England

Soft Pools Of Light

By Mark McKnight

As I sit, I listen for that is what I am paid to do. I do not want to listen and you do not want to speak but we must continue with this charade so that we both may pay our bills.

As I sit, I begin to notice the light. For today, the light is destroying me; the harsh, reality of the sunlight that burns upon me in this afternoon haze. This light is the destroyer. It is fire. It is destruction. This light will tear me apart. It has already begun to claw at my face, dragging its sharp nails across my cheek and down my neck.

As I sit, you shift your stance, placing your body in front of the millions of tiny bullets of light that are slowly attacking me. The brief rest is divine but in time, you move again leaving me without defence.

As I sit, the light begins to change. Softer, until I don't notice it any more. It is still warm but it is no longer the destroyer. When your shadow falls on my face once more, I miss the soft caress of this new light. I am cold without it – like a drug, I am dependent on it to make it through the day.

As I sit, the light continues to change. Not in colour or brightness. Rather, the rays of light begin to bend in on one another. Everything slowly, almost imperceptibly becomes a blur. The smooth lines of this world beginning to smudge towards something else that I have only seen on the edge of a dream.

As I sit, everything begins to grow darker. This happens more and more as the years wear on, watching, waiting for them to appear. You are still there. You still talk to me but you know that the light will soon be gone. You do all you can to keep the light in the room but this is a vain quest.

♠◇♣♡

As I sit, finally they appear. The soft pools of light where there once was the harsh reality of afternoon sunlight. Sound is stifled by the darkness surrounding these soft pools – nothing outside them is of any consequence. What is inside them is the whole world. What is outside them is nothing. This is the moment that life is created. Between two worlds I sit, waiting for the coming show – an explosion or an implosion of reality: either way a stunning display. Many times I have witnessed the soft pools explode. Many more times I have seen reality dissolve into nothingness.

As I sit, this ecstasy must come to an end. Soon, the scarlet blush descends on these soft pools of light. Time and space are imploding and the now ruby red light begins to fail. Shapes disappear and the world is recognisable only by patches of light and dark and even the borders between these two antitheses begin to fade into a single colour.

As I sit, there is darkness.

2.11.05
Brompton, England

♠◇♣♡

Empty Cupboards, Empty Life

By Mark McKnight

Like Old Mother Hubbard, when I go to the cupboard, all I see is emptiness. In my kitchen I have precisely ten cupboards. They are all full to overflowing with nothing. I use only one of the cupboards in my kitchen and the rest are left to the wandering mice and for the debris of a life spent too long on the road.

My living room has a sofa, donated by a neighbour and a cheap bookcase made of unfinished wood. There is no television. There is no stereo. There is no DVD player, Xbox or satellite TV receiver. There is me, a gas fire and the wreckage that has never been tidied away ever since I moved in – the advantage of being a bachelor is that there is no urgency to having an orderly house. After all, I know where everything is. Tidying would just confuse me.

My spare bedroom is adrift with the debris of a past life. Two suitcases full of the junk that I have never been quite sure what to do with. Old projects, half finished, that will never be completed. Yet I hesitate to throw them out – they have cost me too much to abandon entirely. The built in wardrobes of this spare bedroom remain empty – I have nothing to put in those cupboards either. More emptiness.

The swamp of my bedroom presents itself twice a day – when I rise in the morning and when I retire in the evening for those are the only times I have call to enter my bedroom. Clothes litter the floor of this room – graded according to when the last time they were worn. Washing day is an occasional treat – a trip across the road to use a kindly neighbour's washing machine and tumble dryer.

Yet I persist in this single man's paradise, a captive to my own foolishness. Every day I look at my empty cupboards and am reminded of what should be there – the flotsam and jetsam that gathers around a life more ordinary. I am reminded of what my life may be had I made other choices or taken another direction.

♠◇♣♡

Even now, the clutter is beginning to gather around my life. For the first time, I own such mundane items as a microwave, a kettle and a toaster (not working). Is escape possible? Will I be able to extract myself from this self inflicted prison?

Fear not – I can see light at the end of the tunnel. Amidst all of the council tax, electricity bills, electoral registers and final demands for overdue gas payments, there is hope. For this is only temporary. I can feel the wanderer within my spirit even now growing restless. There will come a time when abandonment of all this will be the only solution. My heart will soar once more and I will fly far from this place, back to the land and the people I love. If only I knew where this home I long for really is...

7.11.05
Brompton, England

The Girl In The Pink Dress

By Mark McKnight

I had a dream last night about a girl in a pink dress. The most beautiful girl I have ever seen, in my dream I knew she was the girl I was destined to marry. Those eyes, that hair, her smile and her sweet red lips. And that dress. I sure do like her style! Is this a prophecy? Is this really the girl I will marry?

As I wake, I already begin to forget. Like a vapour in the wind, her image starts to melt from my mind. By lunchtime, the whisper of a memory is all that remains in this mind of mine. I try but I can no longer picture that sweet countenance. Only a half forgotten image of the dress she wore remains. Only half remembered – if I were asked to describe it, I could not. But if I saw someone wearing that same pink dress, I would recognise it immediately. All day I try to remember her face but it is futile.

So I am left to search everywhere in this world for the girl in the pink dress. I may recognise her face but I will know her by the dress she wears. Once in the two years since I dreamed that dream did I imagine that I saw the girl in the pink dress. Through a car window as a girl drove past – a girl who I would marry tomorrow if she asked. But she knows not of my affections and at any rate, it was not the dress. I was mistaken.

But it is more than a dress – the dress represents a lifestyle, a way of life that part of my being longs for and another part fears more than anything else in this world. The pink dress represents every hope and fear I have for my life. Every hope I have had for marriage, a family and a so called normal life. Every fear of the abandonment of the lifestyle to which I have become accustomed.

Occasionally still the girl in the pink dress haunts my dreams. I have never seen her face again. In the skewed reality of half sleep, I am unable even to observe the color of her hair or even of her skin.

♠◇♣♡

Just her pink dress burning into my sub conscious, tempting me and taunting me in its own cruel way.

In waking hours, we have the luxury of choosing our thoughts. At night, our dreams choose us. The girl in the pink dress chose me. Treading across my pillow and through my dreams, leaving footprints across my psyche. But the snowstorm of consciousness soon covers these footprints leaving me to guess what these markings on the ground may mean.

And as I wake once more, the memory again begins to fade into oblivion. The pattern and cut of the dress forgotten, replaced with a vague knowledge of a thought of a memory of a daydream of a dream of the girl in the pink dress.

29.10.05
Brompton, England

Limbo

By Mark McKnight

Every fibre of my being wants to scream out, "Why? Why? Why? Why? Why? Why? Why? Why? Why? Why?" What did I do to deserve this blot on my life that has wrenched my heart into pieces?

Two weeks ago, my husband and I were the happiest people in the world. As the bible says, I was 'greatly with child,' meaning that I was huge and about to pop. My pregnancy had been textbook – no problems or anything to worry about. I cried when I had my first scan and saw the baby's heart beat. It was such a special moment. I couldn't have been happier.

My labour was short and sweet – all the better for the epidural sticking out of my back! But as I was delivering my baby boy, somehow the umbilical cord wrapped around his neck. All of a sudden, there was panic in the delivery room. Doctors, nurses and midwives with worried looks on their faces screaming to each other in a language that I didn't understand. Within minutes it was over. My baby was stillborn – choked by the very cord that kept him alive inside my womb.

I did not realise to begin with – I wanted to hold my baby but my husband, my rock explained what had happened. Instantaneously, the tears started to flow. They did not stop for several hours. It was as if all the air was gone in the room. I couldn't breathe. I could feel the emptiness inside me where my baby had been.

And then, just when I thought things could not get any worse, the Holy Roman Catholic Church sent their emissary – the local priest to explain to me about my baby's eternal soul. You see, a Catholic child who dies before he or she is baptised falls between one of the cracks in papal law. They are not recognised by God as being fit for heaven. Their eternal soul must dwell in a place known as 'limbo' –

♠◇♣♡

neither here nor there, heaven or hell. Because of this loophole, there was a problem with burying the child in a catholic graveyard. The child could not be buried with a priest present to read the last rites.

This was the one moment in my life when I needed the church to stand beside me, to understand what I was going through and to say something that would actually be of comfort to me. And what did they do? When I was down, they kicked me in the back. And so my child was buried at night without a priest. All I could think of was my aunt when I was a child telling my mother, "'Tis a shameful thing to have an unbaptised child."

God can have his bloody church. After all that has happened these past few days, I don't think there is a God. I used to. At least I think I did. But an all powerful God would never let this happen. Why? Why? Why? Why?

14.11.05
Brompton, England

Don't Jack!

By Mark McKnight

"Good morning class, it's good to have you...Jack, don't do that...it's good to see you again after your holidays. I hope you all... Jack, it's a little early in the day to be getting into trouble...had a lovely time when you were off school. Maybe if there's time...Jack, please don't use that kind of language in my class...we can tell each other about our holidays...Jack!...after playtime.

The first thing we need to do is...Jack, I don't think licking the chair is a very good idea...mark the register. Let's see who is here shall we?

Alicia...Jack!
Adam...Jack, don't put that drawing pin up your nose.
Bethany...Jack?
Nathan...Jack?
Abigail...Jaaaaack?
Annemarie...JACK!!!

OK, this is silly. I'll finish this off later. Shall we do some...Jack, that's not for eating...numbers? Today we want to learn our...Jack, this is not a dental surgery. Please leave Nathan's teeth alone...two times table. Let's say them together...

One times two is...Jack, please take the pencil out of your ear.
Two times two is...No, Jack – don't put it up your nose either.
Three times two is...Jack, that's disgusting – don't put it in your mouth as well.
Four times two is...Let's not put it in Abigail's mouth either.
Five times two is...JACK! Pencils are not to be used as weapons.
Six times two is...Thank you Jack. Let's see you sit smartly for a while, shall we?
Seven times two is...Jack?

♠◇♣♡

Eight times two is…Where did Jack go?
Nine times two is…Jack? Did anyone see where he went?
Ten times two is…JACK! Don't put your head under the water.
Eleven times two is…Jack, I'm going to get angry in a moment.
Twelve times two is…JACK! I'll ask you nicely one more time. Sit down, fold your arms and sit smartly. I will not ask you again.

Jack, I really mean it this time. Do you want me to send you to the headmaster? That's much better. Do you think you can keep this up until lunchtime?"

Some years later, Jack has calmed down considerably and is practicing his times tables with another teacher…

Teacher: One times two?
Jack: Take the pencil out of your ear…
Teacher: Two times two?
Jack: Don't put it up your nose either…
Teacher: Three times two?
Jack: Don't put it in your mouth now as well…
Teacher: Four times two?
Jack: Let's not put it in Abigail's mouth either…
Teacher: Five times two?
Jack: Pencils are not to be used as weapons…
Teacher: Six times two?
Jack: Let's see you sit smartly for a while, shall we???
Teacher: Seven times two?
Jack: Jack???
Teacher: Eight times two?
Jack: Where did Jack go???
Teacher: Nine times two?
Jack: Did anyone see where he went???
Teacher: Ten times two?
Jack: Don't put your head under the water…
Teacher: Eleven times two?
Jack: I'm going to get angry in a moment…
Teacher: Twelve times two?
Jack: Sit down, fold your arms and sit smartly!

What are we to do? The government still can't understand the poor number skills of our country!

7.10.05
Northallerton, England

Memphis, Tennessee

By Mark McKnight

I can't leave this country yet. There is one more thing I must do before I depart. Although I haven't seen a familiar face for over two weeks now, I must go to Memphis and visit Gracelands.

I have been an Elvis fan all my life. I even have a little shrine to Elvis in my bedroom. My husband thinks I am totally crackers but he doesn't understand. Elvis was the only man in my life who never let me down. His music was my only way to escape from the misery of my teens and the drudgery of my twenties. So now that I am an 'older' woman, it is time for me to visit his home. Gracelands, the house made famous by the one, the only Elvis Presley.

I left the Mississippi delta on a train going north and arrived in Memphis late on a Tuesday night in June. Where else could I stay but the Heartbreak Hotel? There were no tears on my pillow that night, unlike the hundreds of nights that I cried over Elvis as a teenager.

On Wednesday morning, I rose early and boarded the courtesy bus to take me to Gracelands. I always thought this moment would have more romance about it. A cheery driver in a red blazer and shiny brass buttons carried us up the drive and my dream became a reality.

Looking back, I really can't remember much about it. I remember the jungle room, a place I had only heard about and dreamed about. In my dream, I would wait there and Elvis would join me. It was never sexual. We just talked. But I know it made a difference just being there.

When I got back, I had all kinds of souvenirs to add to my shrine – pictures, key chains and even a life sized Elvis cardboard cutout – I don't know how I ever got it onto the plane. Now I see that I need to keep remembering him and praying for him. If I forget about him, he really will die.

♠◇♣♡

My husband doesn't understand. He says I care more about Elvis Presley than my own husband. But he can't empathise with me. Elvis can – he knows what I've been through. Terence (my husband) says he'll leave if I don't get rid of all this junk. He says it's ruining our marriage. I need to make a choice – it's him or Elvis.

Terence…or…Elvis???

Terence…or…Elvis???

…

…

…

…

Terence…or…Elvis???

I can't make this decision. Which one do I need the most? Which one needs me the most? Maybe going to Gracelands was a bad idea. How can I say that? It is the only place I have ever felt safe – where men can't harm me.

I have taken apart my shrine. I have seen sense and chosen my husband over Elvis Presley. Instead, I am devoting my attention to redecorating. I have decided that our living room needs a makeover. It's going to have a jungle theme.

1.11.05
Brompton, England

The Curse Of Scotland

By Mark McKnight

In a standard deck of cards, a variety of cards have meanings or historical significance. The nine of diamonds is one such card, known as the Curse of Scotland ever since an English king wrote the order to attack on this same card. What you need to understand is the long standing animosity between England and the celtic nations of Ireland, Scotland and Wales. You will see this in any major international sporting event where the Irish, Scottish and Welsh are happy to cheer for each other but <u>NEVER</u> for England.

So it's time for the Scots to get militant. For too long, the Irish have been hogging the limelight in their fight for freedom using the ballot box and the armalite (a favourite slogan of the IRA).

My name is Bill and I am a Scottish loyalist. My demands are simple: a free Scotland, free from the tyranny of English rule. My campaign will be conducted solely by peaceful means. I will not use violence in my righteous crusade. For centuries, too many Scots have died at the hands of the English. I am Martin Luther King Jr. I am Mother Theresa. I am Mahatma Gandhi.

I will conduct my campaign under ground for although my means are peaceful, I am devious nonetheless. My first quest in which I urge you to join is the defacement of every nine of diamonds that I come across. I will carry a black marker to every card game and mark a black cross signifying death on the nine of diamonds. Death to English oppression, death to government by a foreign power and in memory of all those brave Scots who have died at the hands of the British. This shall be our first deed: first blood from what must and will be a long and at times hopeless battle.

Our hero in this quest shall be the hero of Scotland, William Wallace. He alone represents all that is true and noble about Scotland. Like William Wallace, I will yell 'Freedom' in the face of the English.

♠◊♣♡

This occupying force who have infiltrated the very fabric of our society will know that Scotland will no longer stand for it. We will stand as one and shout 'Freedom' from every rooftop. Our streets will resound with the cry. And every time they play cards, they will see a black cross on the nine of diamonds as a lasting reminder of their numbered days.

'Aha!' I hear you cry. Scotland already has a devolved government. Patsies for British indecision and apathy about our fair land. A Scottish parliament that is consistently over budget and over rated. Their decisions are irrelevant. This is a puppet parliament for continued English oppression.

Mark my words, the British government as an occupying force is here to suppress you and take your taxes. They lie to you – it says so in the newspapers. You just need to know how to read them. It is English oppression, that's what it is.

14.11.05
Brompton, England

♠◇♣♡

Since 3:48 This Afternoon

By Mark McKnight

Since 3:48 this afternoon, these clothes no longer suit my lifestyle. And that is the reason I have removed my tie, unbuttoned my shirt and taken off my shoes. For this is now the holidays. I am off to climes more pleasant to rise early that I may watch the dawn and while away the balmy summer evenings sipping on cold drinks on the veranda of my summer residence.

Maybe I shall stay. I choose to remain where my heart is. Why should I migrate like the birds of the air? Six short weeks to sooth my soul, only to return to this land that is neither Ireland nor Africa.

At 3:48 this afternoon I drove home barefoot, as a reminder of those sweet Californian days when cares were few, or at least with fewer cares than now.

Since 3:48 this afternoon, I have been packing my belongings – the lease has run out on my winter residence. I am forced to find a new home once again – a wanderer with only one place to call my own. I shall wait a while, to see what tomorrow may bring. Four million dollars may come may way. Or more debts. Who knows what a day may bring? I am forced to find a new home but I fear I will only find a residence and not a home. I will leave this misery for my return.

Since 3:48 this afternoon, I have been checking my passport and tickets. Knowing that I am ready to go but fearful of what I leave behind. What will there be for me to return to? For now I care little. I bid a farewell to those from whom I am departing and board the silver bird to carry me home. A fonder salutation is ready for those who will find me in my true home.

With prayers seemingly unanswered, nothing stops the relentless rise and fall of the orbs of day and night in the heavens. All too soon, I am forced to depart from my family once again and put on

♠◇♣♡

the shirt, tie and shoes – the symbols of my past choices that have led me here.

This time, no comfort awaits in the land of my sojourn. When will I once again be homeward bound? But I am an optimist. Maybe this year or maybe the next or even after that, I will be permitted to return to my people. To find a bride amongst my people and raise a family of my own. To be baptised into the faith of my fathers amongst my family and the people I love.

Since 3:48 this afternoon, and every afternoon, I long for my return to the dusty, arid land where I should have been born. There will come a day when, at 3:48 in the afternoon, I will once again remove my tie, unbutton my shirt, take off my shoes and drive home barefoot, rejoicing in the knowledge that I am once again going home.

28.10.05
Brompton, England

♠◇♣♡

Porn Star

By Mark McKnight

Let's face it. Morality and money are not two independent concepts. I guarantee, if you were offered enough money to do something, regardless of your 'moral stance,' you would do it.

I make my money from the 'glamour' business. I happen to be a very beautiful woman that makes her money by taking her clothes off. Do I make much money? Damn right I do!

Everyone asks me about the moral dilemma of taking my clothes off for money. I tell them, there's no dilemma. With the money I make for getting naked and having a few photos taken, I can afford my nice apartment, my nice car, nice holidays, nice clothes and nice meals at nice restaurants. Believe me, I have no moral dilemma. Every now and then some fundamentalist will shout abuse at me. Apparently, I'm polluting the minds of children and what do I think God thinks about me doing what I do? Well, to be fair, God is the one who gave me this body. That's right: it's all natural baby! So why shouldn't I use it every way I can? It sure beats the heck out of working for a living.

A lot of men seem to get confused about what I do for a living. They see my picture in a newspaper or a magazine and think I'm a sure thing. They think I'm easy. You see, that's the difference between me and the seedier end of our business. I'm a glamour model. Not a prostitute. I don't have sex for a living – I just take my clothes off. It might be voyeuristic but I love what I do.

I don't touch the internet stuff at all – those guys are just too weird. Always wanting you to do the weirdest things. Some of the new breed of men's mags get a bit raunchy at times but they're all very tongue in cheek and I really enjoy the photo shoots so I tend to do lots of those. The old school of smutty mags like Playboy and Mayfair

♠◇♣♡

don't pay as well as they used to – the internet has taken away all their business I think.

Would I ever do any of the internet stuff? I already told you – that stuff is just too weird. They want you to do all kinds of kinky stuff that apparently turns men on. No way. It's just not for me. I don't do sex – I told you, I'm a glamour model – mostly topless stuff. Let me show you my portfolio – some of these are pretty old. I have a few magazine cuttings from features I've been in.

No way. Forget it. I'm not interested in that kind of stuff. Of course, if the price was right…

Well why didn't you say so to begin with. If we're talking about that kind of money, you can get whatever kind of party you want baby. Oh, uh…that's going to cost you extra. I'm looking forward to doing business with you.

7.11.05
Brompton, England

♠◇♣♡

A Day Late And A Dollar Short
By Mark McKnight

An old man walks along a long, straight road. The burdens of his world weigh him down: shoulders hunched, back stooped. A man who has seen his share of troubles in this world. Not blessed with the gift of oration or academic excellence or the classically chiselled jaw of a model, this man has lived his life perpetually in the shadow of another. Always second best, his achievements were always eclipsed by another. An also ran in the worst sense of the word.

As he walks along this dusty road, going nowhere in particular, he thinks (as he does every day) of his one shot at greatness. At this time of year, the dust is so thick and so dry that his bare feet leave deep imprints on the ground behind him. But his one and only chance to create something better than himself went the same way as everything else in his life: he just came up a day late and a dollar short.

As he thinks of each of the painful disappointments of his life: when his wife left him, when he was made redundant, when his son was killed in a car crash, he remembers the crushing pain that almost destroyed him. He remembers not being able to breathe. He remembers the feeling of emptiness that seemed to grow with every passing day. As he thinks, he imagines the pain bearing down on his shoulders and imagines his feet making deeper imprints in the dust from the devastating weight of the burden that he carries.

This pain was not a pain that came from any simple kind of grief or loss. This was a pain that was much worse. This pain came from glimpsing what might have been and then having it wrenched from within our grasp: a perfect family, a great job and everything that came with it had been stripped away. All that was left was an empty shell and a knot of all the pain, hatred, malice and discontent that had been allowed to fester and grow every day. Where there should have

♠◇♣♡

been love, there was hate. Where there should have been compassion, there was now only a cold, cold heart.

The wind suddenly whips up and the man has to tie his handkerchief around his mouth and nose to prevent him breathing this vile dust. But the wind does not last long. After a few minutes, the wind dies down as suddenly as it started.

The man has reached the top of a long, gentle slope. As he looks back along the road, he notices the footprints. They must have been part way covered up by the dust and the wind. He sees how some footprints are deeper than others. It was as if someone had helped him carry his burden for some of the time – the times when he had been thinking about the worst type of pain from throughout his life. As he turns to leave, he sees the man…

12.11.05
Brompton, England

Tourette's For The Under Tens

By Mark McKnight

He is a normal child in almost every way. He began to walk and talk and crawl and eat solid foods right around the time he was meant to as a baby. I played him Mozart because that's meant to help a baby. But most of all, I loved him more than any mother has ever loved her son. He is my world – my everything. Until he started school, we never suspected that anything was wrong. He was our bundle of joy and nothing could spoil our happiness. All I ever wanted was for him to be a normal kid.

A few weeks after he began school, his teacher asked for a meeting after school. She said my baby has 'special educational needs' whatever that means. She talked way too fast with words that I didn't understand. I was scared – what was going on? I'm sorry to admit that I cried. The teacher was very supportive and went through it all, explaining what everything meant. She explained what the implications would be for my son. That he would get the help that he needed but that he would always be one step behind the rest of the class.

I was devastated. My baby wasn't normal. As he began to grow up, his problems became more apparent as the gap widened between him and his contemporaries. The worst part of it was that they began to diagnose what was wrong with him. Dyslexia. Dyscalculia. It was almost as if my baby couldn't learn. They tried all kinds of programs and ideas to try to help him learn but it was as if none of them helped.

The most unsettling was Tourette's Syndrome. He would be sitting as peaceful as could be but then he would suddenly burst out with a string of swear words. Then he would go right back to what he had been doing. His teacher just seemed to take this in her stride but it really broke my heart. At home, he would look me in the eye and his words were filled with hatred and venom as he swore and swore right

♠◇♣♡

to my face. There was nothing I could do to make him stop. Every night I cried my eyes out for the things he had said to me, praying to God that he would just make my son normal.

For God's sake, he's nine years old. My heart breaks that he even knows those words much less uses them. Once in a moment of clarity, he told me that it's like his mouth is doing things that his mind doesn't want to. He gets so frustrated because he just can't stop and that makes him angry. His anger always turns to violence because he knows no other way to express these emotions that rage inside him. I feel so helpless – I just wish there was some way I could help my son. Whatever the price, I would gladly pay to give him a normal life.

1411.05
Brompton, England

Cry Not For Me
For I Am Already Dead

By Mark McKnight

My life is what you might call an inevitability. An unstoppable force, like a steam train speeding to the precipice of a broken bridge. My life destroyed by my life's work.

Many years ago I left school full of big ideas of how I might change the world or at least make life easier for one or two people. Medicine was my chosen profession – I felt therein lay the greatest potential for helping people. And so I studied earnestly until I became the leading expert in my field – the field of preventative and palliative care for patients suffering from HIV/AIDS. A scourge upon the earth, some 'scientists' have vilified our continent for unleashing this horror upon the world. Apparently, it mutated into the human population from monkeys. The insinuation was clear but also unfounded.

The pharmaceutical companies care little for the plight of anyone bar their shareholders so their anti retroviral drugs are all but inaccessible to most except the very rich or very corrupt, a class people there is no shortage of in Africa. Praise God for the NGOs. They do their best to supply us with the drugs we need to treat our patients. That's how my clinic keeps going. I've always felt that to be an expert, one must have constant first hand experience which is why, despite the travelling and the lectures and the conferences, I try to spend at least half my time in my own clinic, treating patients.

Every day I watch people die – emaciated, weak, forlorn. Families with no money for drugs or medical treatment. No money for a proper funeral. Death by AIDS is not pretty when you're taking the ARVs. Without the luxury of the drugs, horror writers couldn't come up with a more miserable way to die.

Mine is a dangerous profession. Exposure to AIDS, hepatitis and all manner of infectious diseases comes on a daily basis. A slipped

♠◇♣♡

needle, a sloppy movement of the scalpel can be the difference between life and death for both patient and physician. The only difference is that usually it takes the physician much longer to die than the patient.

And thus is my case. Having dedicated my life to caring for AIDS patients, I have contracted that same infection. In attempting to ease the convulsions of an AIDS patient in his final death throes, the needle delivering the sweet release of morphine also pricked my own skin. So I shall die just like the hundreds of patients who have died on the wards of my own clinic. Of course, I will be afforded the best care that money can buy and a potent cocktail of drugs to slow the onset of full blown AIDS and eventually death. But eventually, die I shall – another victim of a plague, a judgement on mankind for his apathy. This cursed body already wracks with pain. I may have days, I may have weeks, months or even years. Yet cry not for me for I am already dead.

19.9.05
Northallerton, England

Basketball

By Mark McKnight

The only thing that gives me pleasure in this life is basketball. I live for basketball. Somebody once told me that if the first thing you can think of in the morning is singing, then you should be a singer. Working on the same logic, I'm going to be a basketball player. There's nothing else I could do.

Before I go to school in the morning, I'll shoot a few hoops just to make sure I'm warmed up. I'll play with my friends on the yard before the bell rings for the start of the school day. At recess and lunch, I'm not that worried about eating. I would rather spend my time practising my skills. You see, one day, I'm going to get drafted to the NBA. Hopefully I'll be picked up by the Lakers and play with Shaq and Kobe. I've lived in LA all my life and my pop and I have been going to games since I can remember. Nothing would make him prouder than watching me play in the play offs for the Lakers.

At the end of High School, I got a full basketball scholarship to the University of Berkeley. Basically a free ride. All I had to do was play ball and go to the occasional class and I could party my way through college. I loved every minute of it – the frat parties, the step shows, the freshman mixers with cute freshmen and most of all the basketball. NCAA ball is a big step up from high school basketball but I loved every minute of it – playing with all those great players that I had watched on TV. And I was good. Coach said I was sure to make the draft when I graduated. There were always scouts at matches and at training sessions and it wasn't long before my name was fairly well known in basketball circles as an up and coming dead cert 3-point shooter.

♠◇♣♡

When I graduated college, it came time for the NBA draft. This was the moment I had dreamed about my whole life. College had been a blast but now I was ready to play ball for a living. This would be a dream come true. My name came up in the first draft. For the Hornets. Were they kidding? The Hornets? I barely even know where they are from. New Orleans? What the hell is in New Orleans? What about the Lakers? I've waited my whole life to play for the Lakers. It's all I've dreamed about since I was seven years old. It was going to be perfect. I was going to get drafted to the Lakers, marry my girlfriend Tiffany and then settle down in the Valley to raise a family.

Everything is ruined now. I don't want to go to New Orleans. My life is here in LA. Tiffany hasn't graduated yet. Please don't let your son dream of joining the NBA. It is a wretched wish and a dead end delusion.

14.11.05
Brompton, England

♠◇♣♡

Kikoi Girl

By Mark McKnight

There's this bar that we went to last night. We kind of stuck out, being the only white guys in the place, but our money is just as good as anyone else's on the pool table. To play, there's a chalk list on the wall. Pay your money, sign your name at the bottom of the list and wait your turn. If you win, you get another game. If you can keep winning, you can keep playing. We only arrived in town yesterday after two days in a bus going half way across Africa. So a pint of imitation Guinness and a night's craic with the boys was just what was needed. And I had this incredible run of luck – six games in a row, which turned me into something of a local celebrity. So that's how Diner's Club became our 'local.'

That's also why we're back in the same bar tonight. And why we were all greeted by name when we came in the door by the barmaids and the locals. But things have changed since last night. You see, tonight there's a tournament going on. Of course, as the local pool hustler, I'm obliged to play. But my run of luck has gone and I'm out after my first game. Oh well, easy come, easy go. The other players, recognizing my considerable talent, are keen that I referee their games.

But there's a big problem. You see, there's this girl across the other side of the bar room. Wearing figure hugging blue jeans and a kikoi (a traditional tribal wrap), she is incredibly beautiful and she's over there dancing by herself. My buddies have noticed that I'm interested. 'Are you going to go over and talk to kikoi girl,' they are asking. And I'm thinking about it. Seriously. I'll maybe go over once this game is over – I can't leave in the middle while I'm refereeing. I can certainly check her out from afar while I'm standing here though.

What? What are you arguing about? There's some kind of problem with the pool game. Somebody wants two shots for something. What do I think? I don't know, my eyes were firmly fixed

48

♠◇♣♡

on kikoi girl. Yes sir, she's incredible. I'm the referee? Oh, bugger! Errr...let me see...no, only one shot. Oops, wrong answer. Things are in danger of getting physical here...I better stick with my decision. Otherwise they'll know I wasn't paying attention. It was a close call anyway, wasn't it? My friends are looking at me with those 'can't believe it' eyes. The players are looking at me with those 'I'm going to f**king kill you' eyes.

And then the fight breaks out. Only they have pool cues and I don't. My friends are off their seats to back me up. Everyone is on their feet – trying to fight or else trying to stop other people fighting. I can't see kikoi girl. What? Let's get out of here? Now? Good call. What about kikoi girl? Oh, bugger!

9.9.05
Northallerton, England

Hooligan!

By Mark McKnight

What a season. This is why they call it the beautiful game. The F.A. Cup is every non-league side's dream. To win the F.A. Cup against Arsenal or Chelsea or Manchester United is the romantic delusion of anyone who has ever played for their local team.

I've been a Darlington supporter all my life. We've had our ups and downs but for now, things have been down for a few seasons. That's why we're a 'conference' team – not good enough for the proper leagues, not bad enough to be labelled as non-league.

But this year, with the big African up front, the Kiwi on the wing and the ugly Frenchman in defence, things are back on the up. Not in the conference, I hasten to add but in the F.A. Cup.

What a whirlwind – all season, better teams forgot how to play football in the Williams Motors Stadium. And that is how we find ourselves facing the might of Chelsea in the Millennium Stadium in the F.A. Cup final.

In the ground, the fans are segregated. No such luxury is afforded in the bars. There's a man beside me at the bar. His face filled with hatred and jealousy. "Darlo have no right to be here! A conference team has no business playing football against us. They are going down. There's no two ways about it." Of course, his shirt was blue. Darlo's moment of glory was not to be ruined by a lone voice of contempt and nothing could dampen our spirits.

As we entered the ground, our hearts swelled with pride. Our Darlington. In the F.A. Cup final. At length, the game commenced and from the outset, it was clear that it was to be a scrappy game. Both teams came to the pitch with fire in their eyes and the first half was defined by fouls, seven yellow cards and no goals.

The second half fared no better with a fight between players, two red cards and one player dispatched to casualty. The game was

♠◇♣♡

held scoreless until the final whistle. Extra time was gut wrenching with play up and down the pitch, a bunch of fine chances.

In the last minute of extra time, an iffy penalty was awarded to Darlo. Both sets of fans were restless. Even from the video evidence, it is debatable which fans were on the pitch first. The penalty was never taken. The police desperately tried to keep the London fans away from the just as zealous Darlington supporters.

But like the unstoppable force meeting the immovable object, the riot began. We threw chairs, coins, batteries and anything we could find at them. They threw them right back at us. My head was cut and bleeding but it didn't matter. I had to defend Darlington's honour. No London poser was going to ruin Darlo's moment of greatness.

In the end, the match was abandoned. Our teams were punished – third and fourth battled for the title. We had destroyed our own moment.

1.11.05
Brompton, England

A Wife's Dilemma

By Mark McKnight

I am torn between what I know is right on the one hand with what I know is right on the other. On the one hand, the unquestioning support of my husband which is the right thing to do – that's what a spouse should do. On the other, to question the honesty and integrity of the one I love publicly by telling the police what I now know which is the right thing to do – that's what any citizen should do.

I had suspected for a while now that all was not as it should be. My husband is the pastor of a medium sized church which does all right. But not that well. He has always driven a really nice car, we live in a lovely house and we're what I would call 'cash rich.' We're not rolling in it but if we ever want or need something, there's always money there to pay for it.

As a young woman, I never questioned this or thought about it – we were just fortunate. But then I began to hear whispers in the church and notice things that I hadn't before. My husband would be evasive when I spoke about where all the money came from. I'm fairly sure pastors don't get paid as much as we seem to have. He sometimes referred to a mystery trust fund from his rich great uncle.

Since our bank account was in both our names, I decided to investigate a little further. I know it was a little underhanded but I went through some of the papers in his desk and some things just didn't seem to add up. Financial transactions on church accounts that seemed pricey, particularly those involving large sums of cash like a plumber paid $2,000 for one day's work. Our own account had a deposit of $1,500 two days later. There were a couple of other transactions I found of a similar nature, all involving amounts greater than a thousand dollars.

As the pastor's wife, I am the head of the grapevine, the gossip tree that is in every church. So when I see and hear whisperings

♠◇♣♡

that never reach me, I know that something is up. A pastor's wife must pick her friends carefully and the one person who I feel I can trust has told me the nature of these murmurs – the congregation are beginning to suspect that money is going missing and they think it may be the pastor. Of course, nobody has any evidence of this at the moment. Except for me.

He is my husband, my provider, the man I love and the man that loves me, despite his weaknesses and flaws. How can I turn him in? But he is a criminal. He has abused the trust of hundreds of people, including me. How could I do anything but turn him in? I am torn between what I know is right on the one hand with what I know is right on the other.

12.11.05
Brompton, England

Donkey Sanctuary

By Mark McKnight

Once again I am baffled by the seeming inconsistencies of this life for I have just seen my first donkey sanctuary. Now I don't begrudge the donkeys their sanctuary – after all, they are beasts of burden and they deserve to be put out to pasture to enjoy their lazy days of retirement when they are no longer fit for work. The days between the farm and the glue factory are precious few.

What concerns me is not so much the donkey sanctuary as the environs of the aforementioned refuge. You see, this safe haven for old donkeys is situated on the island of Lamu, probably the number two tourist destination on the African coast of the Indian Ocean. Lamu is a so-called island paradise – white sand beaches and crystal clear waters. I've been to some other 'island paradises' and it's the same wherever you go. The tourist areas are incredible: immaculate streets, brightly painted buildings and festive decorations everywhere. But you won't need to walk far before you discover the seedier side of an island paradise. The side that the tourist board doesn't want you to see: houses that are all but falling down, red light districts, dirt roads and abject poverty.

The Bahamas, Lamu, Zanzibar, Easter Island, they are all the same. A few blocks of the most incredible hotels in the world and the rest of the island slaves to the tourism industry: the wages are meagre but the alternative is nothing at all. Nassau was the worst. It took just a single wrong turn down a back alley and I was in the slum.

But back to the donkey sanctuary; my hotel laid on a shuttle service to take a group of us to the site – it's one of the main tourist attractions around here. There was no avoiding driving through the slums – there's only one paved road on the island. Although the tour guide tried to keep our attention on the bus so that we wouldn't have to look out the windows, my mind couldn't help wandering. Children

♠◇♣♡

were begging at the side of the road. Old people sat in doorways, clearly unable to move anywhere. They would probably sit in the same doorway until they died. Here, people *have* to look after each other. There's no such thing as an old people's home. But when you have no money, there's not much you can do for an old relative: can't pay for medicine, can't pay to make your house more comfortable and can't pay even for food. These people scratch out their living as best they can.

On a small island, it doesn't take us long to reach the donkey sanctuary. A triumph of tourism – they have developed interactive displays that explain their work, where the animals come from and everything we want to know about donkeys. That is when the paradox hits me: on this island, the old donkeys are cared for better than the old people. A donkey sanctuary! What a peculiar idea.

12.11.05
Brompton, England

♠◇♣♡

On A Stormy Tuesday Afternoon

By Mark McKnight

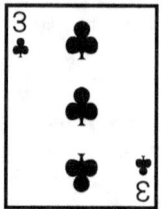

On a stormy Tuesday afternoon, about a year ago, I rolled my car over a hedge. I'll hold my hand up and say it – with a pint of Guinness in me I was going much too fast. It was one of those country roads that twists and turns. I used to really love driving fast: braking hard into the corners and accelerating hard out of them. I went snoring round a corner far too hard, took it too wide and met a car coming the other way. I swerved to miss him and, thank God, I did. Problem was I hit the hedge on my own side of the road, bounced off it, spun round sideways then began rolling properly. My car and I dropped six feet off the edge of the road and I ended up on my roof. A seal on the petrol tank just happened to be broken and so petrol began leaking into the now upside down car.

People stopped to help – made sure that I was out of the car. It wasn't long before this spectacle had gathered something of a crowd – police, onlookers, innocent bystanders and the like. Shame to say there was no explosion – it wouldn't make a very good movie. The policeman took a few statements and organized for a lorry with a crane to get my car out of the field. He talked about getting a fire engine because of the leaking fuel but in the end, they decided they didn't need it. The farmer who owned the field scratched his head for a bit and then asked who would fix his fence that he'd only just built? The onlookers waited until all the excitement was over and then went on their merry way.

After things had all died down, my dad let the rest of my family know who were, as you can imagine, decidedly worried. We thought about keeping it a secret from my mum but it would have to get out sooner or later. My dad also organized to get my car fixed – I mean, how long could I really do without my car. Before I had the accident, I had to use it every day. There was no reason for that to

♠◇♣♡

change. Straighten out the roof, new windscreen, new sunroof, new bonnet, one new door, replace most of driver's side suspension, two new tires, one new wheel rim. He really worked hard to get the car on the road again in next to no time.

I dream about the accident almost every night. It happens in slow motion and I have time to look around and see every blade of grass. I relive it during daylight hours too – every gut wrenching second of it. Over and over again. You see, I never regained consciousness – I survive on life support systems. My family maintain their beside vigil hoping and praying that one day I will wake up.

Do I want to wake up? Could I face them?

26.10.05
Brompton, England

Taxi Jihad

By Mark McKnight

As a human being, I like to see myself as a fairly easy going type of guy. I don't mind most people – if they get on my taxi, pay their money and don't give any trouble then they are basically my friend. As a Moslem, things are a little different. I'm not a smart man. In fact, I never even finished school. I can just about read and write but my mother and father are Muslims so I guess that makes me one too. The imam at the mosque we go to keeps telling us about fatwa and jihad and holy war against the western infidels. I don't really understand it but he says that it is the duty of all Muslims to do what they can do to disrupt the work of the Christian infidels.

First let me clarify. I'm not going to become a suicide bomber or something. I just don't believe in a god that would let someone kill themselves. On the other hand, there are other things I can do to disrupt the lives of these people. That is why I have declared a taxi jihad on anyone with white skin. Here's the way it works. Ordinarily, I am a good driver – I stick to the speed limits and am considerate to other drivers. But if someone with white skin gets in my taxi, I make sure they are sitting up front where they can see everything. Then I drive to put the fear of God in them.

I know this road like the back of my hand. I drive it ten to fifteen times a day so I know the road. I drive on the edge of the road where it falls away to nothing. From the passenger seat, it looks like I'm about to fall off the edge. I don't slow for potholes – I either just bump straight through them or I swerve hard just before I reach them. I drive right on the tailgate of the car in front. I use my horn at every available opportunity. I pretend to get angry with the other drivers. I hang out my window and shout while I don't look where I'm going. Sometimes when the road is quiet, I will pretend to sleep – closing the eye that the white man can see but keeping the other one open. Then I

♠◇♣♡

will begin to drift into the lane of oncoming traffic. Once or twice, the white man has grabbed the wheel and swerved back into my own lane. Usually, I have to pretend to wake up with a start and swerve back onto my own side of the road again. Sometimes I'll mount the kerb when I swerve back. I keep an empty bottle of Waragi in the taxi half filled with water and take a swig of it every now and then.

So far, taxi jihad has been very successful with plenty of tears, screams and some soiled underwear. Taxi Jihad is my contribution to fatwa.

12.11.05
Brompton, England

♠◇♣♡

Ahmed's Emporium

By Mark McKnight

"Ah, welcome, welcome sir. Welcome to Ahmed's Emporium. I beg of you – please, come in, have a look around, make yourself at home. If there is any way I can be of service to you, just let me know. I am here to serve you in whatever way I am able."

Ahmed's Emporium, purveyor of groceries, confectionery, haberdashery and 'fancy goods' according to the sign. This is the base of operations of one of the most sophisticated intelligence operations in the world. Not for a government or a terrorist network. Ahmed's Emporium is the original grapevine. The CIA or MI5 could learn a few things in Ahmed's Emporium. Few people who enter Ahmed's Emporium are unknown to Ahmed for a reputation almost certainly precedes all but the most down at heel in this town.

Ahmed's Emporium is visited by dignitaries, statesmen and politicians on a regular basis for he has what he likes to refer to as his 'special section.' Housed in the basement of the premises, it is here that Ahmed sells his 'fancy goods' – real Irish whiskey. This whiskey could not be described as duty paid and as a result is only available to Ahmed's closest friends, relatives and acquaintances.

A good single malt Irish whiskey is hard to come by in Africa and so Ahmed has many friends. But one does not become Ahmed's friend overnight – time and energy must be devoted to the purchase of a bottle of Bushmills or a half of Paddy. And one does not become intimate with someone like Ahmed without revealing a few personal details about one's own life.

And so Ahmed was privilege to information from his powerful friends that others might pay good money for. On the other hand, Ahmed was one of the few truly incorruptible people. Ahmed would not drink his own whiskey, for drunkards had loose tongues and he knew that careless talk cost lives.

♠◇♣♡

Ahmed's wife was not similarly gifted. For she needed no alcohol to loosen her tongue. But Ahmed knew his wife of old and fed her half truths, vague tales and outright lies to protect her from her own gossip.

On a clement spring evening, Ahmed heard from one of his many friends that the president would die later that night from a heart attack. Ahmed's way was never to question but he thought it odd that someone could predict a heart attack with such accuracy, particularly an enemy of the man.

As the news reports came in after sunset of what had happened, Ahmed knew he was in trouble. For it was not a heart attack that was suspected, rather a murder. Ahmed had knew this day would come – when he knew too much and he put his plan into place. He retrieved the bag that he kept for this purpose – packed with a toothbrush, a razor, a clean shirt and two bottles of Bushmills. He looked around his emporium one last time, locked the door and disappeared into the night.

30.10.05
Brompton, England

♠◇♣♡

Superfluous Beauty Treatments

By Mark McKnight

I walked by the mall yesterday which started me off on an interesting train of thought. You see, they were selling something called a tongue scraper. Apparently, all this gunk builds up on your tongue and the best thing to do is to get one of these scrapers to scrape it all off there. Well really! I mean, tongue scrapers? How on earth did we ever get by without these inventions in the past? The human race has been on the go anything from a few thousand to a few million years, depending on who you listen to. Tongue gunk hasn't wiped us out yet but someone, somewhere has decided that this is the next must have item.

What perturbed me about this was the number of people who were buying them. My wife included. Seemingly sensible and well adjusted people were queuing to buy their very own tongue scraper. Was this symptomatic of a wider problem? What other kinds of things might my wife have bought without my knowledge?

I resolved to wait until my wife's back was turned or for an opportune moment and then I would open her cosmetics drawer – somewhere I had never dared venture for fear of what I may find. I had been so intrigued by the tongue scraper incident, I could stand it no longer.

So this evening, while my wife was at her Spanish class, I very gently slid open the bathroom drawer where my wife stories her 'ladies things': make up, toiletries, etc.

Conveniently, all the potions and lotions had labels on them and I was able to make an educated guess as to their use. One or two bottles left me bemused but that was not what agitated me the most. For the drawer was divided into sections and one section was clearly where my beloved kept her 'tools of the trade:' nail clippers, hairbrush, curling tongs (I had seen these used regularly).

♠◇♣♡

What concerned me was the bewildering array of hardware whose purpose I could not even hazard a guess. Although we enjoy a full and varied sex life, none of these had ever come into play so I was certain that their use was entirely innocent. But what could all these implements possibly be used for? Some were clearly designed for conducting treatments of surgical precision while others included receptacles to be powered by an external supply of electricity. Others looked like accoutrements acquired from the clearance of a Victorian dental surgery.

Despite my own biased opinion, my wife is (by popular acclaim) regarded as a very beautiful woman. Must I believe that many of these tools are responsible for my wife's beauty or is her beauty the gift from God that I until recently believed it to be? And so, not wanting to advertise my naïvety, I resolved to leave all as I found it. To this day, I still don't know what they were for. At least I am now able to recognise a tongue scraper.

28.10.05
Brompton, England

Between The Devil
And The Deep Blue Sea

By Mark McKnight

This bloody pipeline. Death toll so far: fourteen men, three cows, a chicken and two children.

Two winters have passed since the white men arrived with their grand promises. There would be training and jobs for all our men folk, paying in American dollars. There would be money to spare even after we had all built our new concrete and tin houses. Concrete? Anything would be better than the dung and straw bricks that we have to use now!

The process was to have been simple: cut a supply road straight through the bush – as straight as possible. No turns, no deviation. That would cost too much money! The road was to let the trucks through – mechanical monsters bigger than ten elephants. The trucks brought the supplies to build the pipeline: a three foot wide, gleaming metallic atrocity like a silver rope stretched between the devil and the deep blue sea. We were to finish the job: build the last fifty kilometers of pipeline to connect it to the deep blue sea – the port where, they told us, boats bigger than a village would carry their oil away.

For a season, we prospered – the white men always paid on time in cold hard cash. The men left the fields in favor of the pipeline. The squatters moved onto the land to eke out their existence but we were earning so much on the pipeline that we could buy our food instead of needing to grow it like the peasants. We were rich men now!

The white men sent their salesman and we all bought his televisions – they hooked us up to the electric lines that ran with the pipeline. Telephones were next – paying our phone bills to the white men. We even bought our food off the white man. By now, our rag tag

♠◇♣♡

village of a few farms had changed – everyone lived together in one place so the buses could take us to work each morning.

The first sign of trouble came the day the buses didn't show up. There was nothing to do but wait. And the television wasn't working either. The next day, the white men sent their patsy – a dark skinned man in a cheap suit and with an official looking letter in his hand.

Filled with 'we regret to inform you' and 'we are sorry for any inconvenience this may cause,' the letter announced the abandonment of the pipeline, citing political unrest and the current economic climate.

Not just blood, sweat and tears but human life invested in a doomed project. The fourteen men who died, caught in an explosion were an unfortunate accident. Even the three cows, sacred animals to our tribe, caught in the blast are defensible. But we can not and must not ever forget where responsibility lies for two children who chased a chicken into the unfinished pipeline and never returned.

This bloody pipeline! Death toll so far: fourteen men, three cows, a chicken and two children. Net gain: absolutely nothing.

14.8.05
Between Mombasa & Nairobi, Kenya

♠◇♣♡

The Perils Of Suburban Life

By Mark McKnight

My doctor tells me my cholesterol is too high or I eat too much sugar or I don't get enough exercise so I do what he says – eat more sensibly, get a dog so that I will have to take it for walks in the evening. And that is where the problem begins.

One night, as I'm out walking Max (my dog), I walk along a road that I've never been on before. I'm not that far from my house but for some reason, I've never been on this street before. As I idle down the street, letting Max sniff everything he comes across, I often aimlessly look at the houses that I pass.

I am struck by a house on one side. Set back off the road, it seems to have considerable security for a residential property in this sleepy suburb – CCTV cameras, guard dogs, a high security fence and a video entry system connected to the gate.

As I watch with horror, Max has found a way in through a gap in the fence. He seems to be chasing something. Although I stand at the fence and call him, Max has disappeared around the back of the house. It is clear that he is not going to come by himself. I will have to go and fetch him.

I can sense that all is not right with this house. My own house has a burglar alarm but this is ridiculous. Nevertheless, I push the button on the video entry system and soon the small screen flickers to life. An angry looking young man answers my call and I explain what has happened. He grunts and says he will get my dog for me.

As he walks away, the screen does not shut off but remains active. There on the ground I can see two things that make my blood run cold: a gun and a body lying in a slowly widening pool of blood. I stand, frozen to the spot, scared to run and even more frightened to stay. What about Max? Will he face the same fate?

It seems like hours but in reality it was probably just a few moments tick by and the angry young man carries Max to the gate and

♠◇♣♡

hands him over. I thank him and take my leave – briskly walking towards home. I have gone quite some way when I hear the shout – the man has realised that the monitor was still switched on and what I must have seen. All I can do is run, faster than the wind. I wish I had listened more to my doctor but I am ablaze with the adrenaline coursing through my veins.

Arriving home, I turn off all the lights and watch the street to see if he's there. My wife is terrified because I won't tell her what has happened. The dog is barking because he thinks it's a game. But I watch and wait – has he followed me? Am I safe?

6.11.05
Brompton, England

Talk Lots, Say Nothing

By Mark McKnight

E-e-e-e-e-e-emma!!!!!,

It was so wonderful to talk on the phone last night. My mum will go bananas when she sees the phone bill! I can't believe we talked for almost four hours!

So I just thought I'd write you a note to say hi and to see what you're up to today. I have BORING classes and a meeting in the evening where I have to talk about what I did in Haiti. I might as well have been in outer space for all they care but what can I do? I wish you were coming with me to keep me company.

So did you decide on what your favourite food is? It doesn't have to be something wacky like mine (peanut butter and cheese sandwiches) but I think it's important to know – I don't think one can get far in life without a favourite food.

Did you see Mr. Little after school today? He's such a geek. Why would anyone drive such a freaky little car as that one? What is it with teachers? They're just such a bunch of geeks. Sometimes I think they don't want to be cool.

Cool, cool, cool, cool, cool, cool, cool, cool, cool, cool. That's what you are. In a competition of cool people, you would come third. Here's my list...

1. Elvis Presley
2. James Dean
3. You (Emma Milankovic)
4. The Fonz
5. Mr. Little in his geeky car (just kidding!)

So I need to discuss something very serious with you. We need to decide on 'OUR SONG.' Come on, we've been friends for long enough now. We can have a song, right? I was thinking it should be something from the sixties since that's what we always listen to in

♠◇♣♡

your bedroom. I like lists. Here are my top five and you can pick one...

1. Sugar Sugar by the Archies
2. He Ain't Heavy, He's My Brother by The Hollies
3. Come On Eileen by Dexys Midnight Runners
4. Rocking All Over The World by Status Quo
5. If You Think I'm Sexy by Rod Stewart
   Eeeeeeeeuuuuuuggggggghhhhhh!!!!! NO! We do not think you are sexy, Rod. Maybe if I sang it, you might think I'm sexy...

If you think I'm sexy and you want my body, come on baby mmmm mmmm mmmm (can't remember the words!). Hmmm! Maybe not – not singing a song by a wrinkly rocker anyway.

Anyhoo, that's all I have time to write for now because I have to go to my music class. We're learning about rap music with a capital 'C.' Ha Ha. That was funny. I'll see you on the flip flop.

Lots of love, hugs, kisses, etc.
Mark 'The (Insert Nickname Here)' McKnight
xoxoxoxoxoxoxoxoxoxoxoxoxoxoxoxoxoxoxoxo

P.S. I'm going to be on the telly tonight. I'll sleep anywhere when I'm drunk

P.P.S. Life is like a sofa – you never know when someone is going to sit on you.

P.P.P.S. What does PS stand for, anyway?

P.P.P.P.S. In case I don't see you, Happy Wednesday.

1.11.05
Brompton, England

♠◇♣♡

Free As A Bird

By Mark McKnight

All of a sudden, there is this yawning emptiness. In an instant, my life has changed. The moment for which I have waited and anticipated for two years is upon me. Finally, I am as free as a bird. I have served my sentence, done my time. There were times when I thought I wouldn't make it. When times were low and debts were high and I concocted some hair-brained schemes to pull myself out of the mess in which I was embroiled, the only thing that kept me going was this single defining moment in my life.

And now, two years later, I am free as a bird. For two years I have been shackled to three things: my job, my house and my car. Today, the 22nd of July, I have been made redundant, the lease on my rented house has expired and I have sold my car.

So here I stand on a lonely railway platform as dawn breaks. For the first time in my life, I have broken even. I have no money but I don't owe any money either. I am neither a borrower or a lender. So where do I go? What do I do?

I had prepared myself for this moment – was ready for the freedom it would bring, ready for the new challenges and adventures. I had failed to adequately prepare for one thing – how would I use this new freedom?

As I sit on this deserted platform, time stretches out indefinitely before me. The railway tracks serve as a perfect microcosm of the dilemma which I now face. For in one direction is home – the life I have struggled so hard to leave behind, the person that I was but never wanted to be. In the other direction is the rest of the world – ready to be explored, to be whoever I wanted to be, to be who I really am.

There is a third option – to throw myself on the tracks in front of the train. To escape from the pressures pulling on me from both

♠◇♣♡

directions. Of course, I'm not really going to do it – it's just the voyeur inside of all of us that wonders what it would be like.

As the platform fills, I can see that the world is full of people with the same quandary, just different circumstances. A beautiful teenager who doesn't want to be, but is a goth because all her friends are. A businessman with long hair who doesn't want to be but is because that's what society expects. A single mum who doesn't want to be but is because that's the sort of crappy thing that life throws at you. All victims of circumstances or peer pressure or their own folly and half-baked choices.

So I buy a ticket going somewhere I've never been or even heard of. Just to see what is there. To see who I am when I get there. To make a half-baked choice of my own.

2.11.05
Brompton, England

♠◇♣♡

I'm Packing My Bags And I'm Going Back To Ireland

By Mark McKnight

I always said, half joking half seriously, that I would like to go back to Ireland to die. There's an old Irish blessing that finishes with the line, 'May you die in Ireland' and in all my travels, I lived with that as my mantra. When it came time for my life on this revolving rock to finish, I would not hesitate to pack my bags and go back to Ireland.

Death is coming. I can feel it in my bones. Many years have passed now since I contracted the virus that I knew would eventually kill me. I am one of the lucky ones. With anti retroviral drugs, AIDS has been nothing more than an irritating chronic illness. Those days are over. The drugs no longer work and I can feel the disease slowly ravaging my body.

I have led an interesting life. I lived in seven or eight different countries and visited many more. A wandering heart is never settled and I flitted between lands across three continents in search of my true home until I awoke one morning to realise that my home was not an earthly one and my brief stay on this blue and green planet was a mere trifle compared to an eternity spent in the next life where my true home really was or is or will be.

I had three careers: sound engineer, pastor and author. I tried my hand at many more jobs: teacher, cook, musician, entrepreneur, taxi driver, factory worker, engraver and at my lowest ebb flipping hamburgers at McDonald's. Desperate times have called for desperate measures.

I provided for my family throughout our time together by hook or by crook. We were not very rich but we have not wanted for anything. Only once did we rely on benefits but the generosity of friends and strangers alike has often been the hair's breadth between mere under privilege and absolute ruin.

♠◊♣♡

My children are grown – a salesman, a teacher, a doctor and an academic who have made their own ways. None follow my path, which is good – mine has often been a painful one to tread. My wife passed several years ago, before we had the chance to enjoy our retirement together so I never bothered retiring – I thought I would just continue our work for a few more years.

But now I'm getting old. I can't move the same way I used to. My joints are seizing up with the same arthritis that crippled my grandmother. I still have a full head of hair like my grandfather did to the end of his life but it is silver grey all over – Grecian 2000 is no longer a viable option!

My dying wish in this world is to return to the land of my birth, to see the green hills of Antrim and the Giant's Causeway one more time. To feel the cold wind where the Mountains of Mourne sweep down to the sea and truly live one last time.

14.11.05
Brompton, England

♠◇♣♡

Remembrance Day

By Mark McKnight

Ironically, today is Remembrance Day. A day I can never forget. It will be etched on my mind as long as I live. These people, with their ceremonies remembering their soldiers: deaths that were, in a way, justifiable. Deaths for the greater good – a higher cause. Two world wars that should have been fought.

So where does that leave me? The word that the governments use is 'collateral damage.' Civilian deaths that are regarded as accidents of war. Except this is a war that shouldn't have been fought. A war where both sides are to blame. A war where, even if one side triumphs, nobody will win. Not the soldiers, not the civilians, not the politicians.

My grandfather fought and died in the second war. This year, like every year, we went to pay our respects with the rest of the town. Honestly, I was a bit bored. There were the usual speeches, a very somber parade and the mayor flapping about all pompous and ridiculous. But just as they were laying one of the wreaths of poppies, something happened to change all of our lives forever.

So called 'freedom fighters' have been fighting a civil war here for three hundred years now. They claim to be trying to unite the country but so far as I can see, they are just making things worse. We blame them for the problems and they blame us. And everyone throws stones at the 'filth.'

But today, the bastards reached an all time low. Nothing is worth what they did today. For all I care they can go and fuck themselves. At 10:45 this morning, without warning, the Irish Republican Army detonated a huge bomb made from 40lbs of gelignite close to where me and my parents were standing. There was nothing Irish or Republican about what they did and the only thing I can think of that might connect them to the army was that they used explosives.

♠◇♣♡

The policemen and social workers have been offering me tea and sweets and coke all day long now. They tell me that they understand and that everything is going to be alright. SHUT UP! SHUT UP! SHUT UP! SHUT UP! SHUT UP! YOU DO NOT UNDERSTAND AND EVERYTHING IS NOT GOING TO BE ALRIGHT. I was standing between my mum and dad holding their hands. For some reason, the explosion killed them both and I only got minor cuts and bruises. So let me repeat. For all I care, those bastards can go and fuck themselves.

Eleven people died in the explosion. Another sixty three were injured. But for some reason, I survived. Some days I wish I hadn't. Some days, I wish twelve people had been killed.

And now, ten years to the very day later, the perpetrator's political spokesman offers a 'formal apology.' As if that will make it all OK again. Well thank you very much but you know what? For all I care, he can go and fuck himself too.

3.9.05
Brompton On Swale, England

♠◇♣♡

Incarcerated Visionary

By Mark McKnight

Four years? Are you out of your mind? This is something that fucking happened over ten years ago and now you're sending me to prison for four years. Four years? BASTARDS! And you – what kind of a lawyer are you? You said it would be community service or a suspended sentence.

Six Months Later

Life has settled down now to what I suppose it will be for the next four years. If I'm good, I'll get parole after two. Was I bitter? Of course. Who wouldn't be? Fair enough. I suppose I'm guilty.

In prison, you have a lot of time to think. Time to think about what you did. Why you're here. Think about the mistakes you've made in your life. I've sure made some shitty mistakes. That's partly why I'm here

They say that whatever doesn't kill you only makes you stronger. In prison, that counts for double.

I have all these ideas. Sometimes I wake up at night and feel like I'm going to burst. I open my notebook and start writing. Drawing pictures of my ideas, writing stories or songs or just writing for the sake of writing. I need to fill the pages. I need to somehow capture my ideas on paper. Like a dream, sometimes I wake up and they are gone and then I am sad.

Things come to me in dreams and I know that I will never remember them when I am awake. But only ever during lock down. As soon as I leave the four walls of my cell, they are gone. I am fit to explode one moment and when I walk out the door, I am Joe Everybody. Prisoner number 4043/1. In the prison kitchens where I work or on the exercise yard, I try to capture the same thoughts but

♠◇♣♡

they are not there. They do not exist outside the claustrophobic closeness of my cell with its cold walls and stained ceiling.

What will happen at the end of my sentence when I am forced to leave this place? Will the thoughts and ideas cease forever? Will four years be enough to put down on paper everything that is inside of me? Some days I think that even a life sentence would not be long enough to write everything down. Two life sentences? Three?

But there are demons who visit me in my cell too. Sometimes they whisper and sometimes they scream at me but it is always the same message. What if four years is too long and I begin to believe the things that they say? Or worse begin to do the things they tell me? That would surely give me the life sentences I need.

This prison cell is a dual edged blade that cuts both ways. On the one hand my only solace and refuge, the place where I am visited by moments of implausible crystal clarity. On the other crystallising the flashes of insanity that may yet prove to be my undoing.

31.10.05
Brompton, England

♠◇♣♡

Plastic Palm Trees
By Mark McKnight

Honestly, I just don't understand this city. Although it may sound somewhat clichéd, this is a land of contradictions. But the contrasts here are of the most surreal kind. Let me give you an example. This city is almost right on the equator so one might justifiably regard it as tropical. It also lies on the beautiful Indian Ocean coast line. White sandy beaches stretch for miles, interrupted only by the occasional crafty trader (pun intended) who would rather trade than deal in real money. As you might imagine, the top of the beach is lined with palm trees. Those fresh coconuts are hard to beat.

Yet as we ambled down the citadel's main boulevard, what should we encounter but a row of plastic palm trees. Taller than two men, they were glorious in shades of pink, blue and red. I ask you, in a city where palm trees are native, what possible benefit can there be in displaying these polyurethane monstrosities? If these towering objects of ridicule appeared in my native Ireland, one might understand – an emerald isle painted so green by centuries of incessant rain hitting land for the first time after crossing the broad Atlantic. Yes, a plastic palm tree in Lisburn would shine as a beacon to all the world – a beacon of hope that one day God will bless us with a warmer clime, although I fear this is pure wishful thinking.

In this tropical paradise, these vacuum moulded imitations of nature remain proudly on show – a symbol of the sheer futility of it all. And so, as I leave the city for the last time, my enduring memory is the plastic palm trees at the start of my journey.

The Kinshasa Highway is a fool's journey. They say this road that divides Africa in two was responsible for the spread of AIDS around the world. On a bus that will be lucky to make it, I'm headed all the way – from Mombasa to Kinshasa. The number of people who have died on this road does not bear thinking about. If the bandits

♠◇♣♡

don't get you, the driver manages to keep the bus on the road and you can sneak across the border into Congo, you'll still be lucky to make it. Out here, the mosquitoes carry a strain of malaria for which there is no medicine – just a slow and painful death.

But what choice do I have? A white man caught between two worlds. The father of my Congolese wife is dying. His whole working life has been with the ever changing political machinery of the DRC. For a career to last that long in Congo, he's either very powerful, very corrupt or both. Not showing up for his funeral would be a sleight, so here I am on a suicidal journey into the heart of deepest Africa. There's a good chance that I won't return. Tell my mother I love her. And for God's sake, cut down those bloody plastic palm trees.

11.9.05
Brompton On Swale, England

♠♢♣♡

I Killed Summer Fun

By Mark McKnight

We weren't around for the Summer of Love, 1969. A cruel twist of fate meant that the oldest of our group wasn't born until ten years later. That may not have been a bad thing – after all, they say if you can remember it, you weren't there. If none of us can remember it, then we must all have been there, at least in spirit.

So we decided to have our own Summer of Love, 2004. It was in California – the perfect place for a Summer of Love. Problem was, as Christians, the whole free love thing is a bit shaky. So we decided that it would be the Summer of Fun. That would attract less criticism from others.

The Summer of Fun was embodied in one man – the one they call the Sultan of Fun. He was the driving force of Summer Fun. Together, we drank gallons and gallons of whatever we could find, but always using Pepsi as a mixer. The Sultan of Fun would abide no cheap imitations and was vehement in his abhorrence of Coca-Cola. In our old Ford van, we must have covered thousands of miles together in the pursuit of life, liberty and fraternity but most of all to find that one pure experience of the Summer of Fun.

Our summer really began in late spring as the thermometer was beginning to rise after a cold winter in Ireland and a dusty spring in the fields of Africa. When we arrived in California, all seriousness was abandoned in favour of the official Summer of Fun. It began on a cool evening at In 'n' Out Burgers when the Summer of Fun was officially inaugurated between the four of us: The Sultan of Fun, Cyler Middleton (film director), JD Cubillos (from Christian death metal band, Thrash! Amen) and me.

The Summer of Fun meant as much to us as the Summer of Love meant to those who were there back in '69. It was our everything – we carried our guitars on our backs and sang as the sun went down.

♠◇♣♡

We went to San Francisco and hung out at Haight-Ashbury. We were the lone beatniks amongst a sea of faces of every creed and colour, just trying to make it through another day. But the Summer of Fun was about so much more than that.

I alone am responsible for the end of the Summer of Fun. I alone was unwilling or unable to leave the rest of the world behind – responsibilities, problems, issues and relationships unresolved. On a Sunday night in late August, I took the inaugural members of the Summer of Fun for ice cream and announced my intent to leave. Tears followed. Anger, resentment, recrimination. In that instant, the Summer of Fun was over. It was not my departure that killed it but rather that I had entertained the thought of leaving. I had awoken the reality that summer fun was a fickle construct that we had created.

I killed summer fun.

12.11.05
Brompton, England

♠◇♣♡

Pavement Café

By Mark McKnight

Looking back, the revolution could have started in no other place, this pavement café in full view of the world. Sitting at the edge of Africa with all of Mombassa passing by with the relentless stream of taxis along Jomo Kenyatta Avenue. Pedestrians who cared little for our group – just trying to make it through another day.

Every night we visited the same café – eating Shawarma and drinking Scud. To begin with, we waited our turn for space to sit on the benches, squeezing up when more customers came to eat their Swahili food. As time went by, the regulars came to know us, making space for us, appreciating our custom and our patter. After all, the eight burly men who visited every night more or less kept this pavement café afloat with our business.

How I long for those balmy Kenyan evenings sitting out of doors waiting for something, anything to happen. But Mombassa is a city that will take hold of you if one is not careful. It has a mystical enchantment that can make you see things as they are not. Maybe it was the Shawarma or maybe it was the night air, but on a warm summer's evening, our brotherhood decided that tonight was the night for the revolution to begin.

We decided that ours would be a peaceful revolution. Family members lost to Idi Amin, to the IRA, to the LRA, to Chechen rebels. No longer would we stand for these crimes against humanity. Now was our time. We would do something about it. We were the revolutionaries who would change the world. Governments may topple and regimes may come to an end but this was the revolution. It was the only thing pure left in this world. We were the new world order.

At around one in the morning, Mombassa begins to settle down for the night and by then we were ready to formally announce our statehood to the rest of the world. Our constitution (on the back of

♠◇♣♡

a napkin, replete with Shawarma stains) was signed by all parties concerned and we began our march of independence. Right up to the first government building we could find: the Department of Agriculture and Fisheries.

Still on a Shawarma high, we demanded of the guard to see the president who informed us that the president was in Nairobi so far as he knew. He did offer to pass on a message for us so, handing him our constitution we asked him to inform the president of our intent to become and independent state. We planned to annex Mombassa Island first thing tomorrow. The guard seemed to derive much merriment from our plans – come the revolution, he would be the first to go.

The next morning we needed a lie in. Get up at lunchtime. Go for some ice cream and a trip to the beach. It was mid-afternoon before we remembered the revolution. Too late in the day to annex an island – maybe on Monday morning?

28.10.05
Brompton, England

♠◇♣♡

A Proper White Man

By Mark McKnight

Apparently, I'm not a proper white man. This is something that I don't entirely understand. My Irish skin is much paler than the swarthy Californian complexion that my friend Nakyanzi is used to on visitors but yet I have been branded as a misfit. And therein lies the enigma of a life spent too long travelling.

There was a time when Ireland was home. The green hills and the rolling fields – every cliché you have heard is true. But one day, I determined to go and see the world. Problem is, once you go away from home, you never go all the way home (in your mind I mean).

Days turned into weeks and weeks turned into months and next thing I know, it's been two and a half years since I've spent longer than a weekend in Ireland at one time. Is home somewhere else? In my lifetime, I've resided in five different countries. Ireland has already been ruled out as home – we've grown apart all these years, although I still like the romantic notion of going back there to die and become worm food in the damp earth of my birthplace. (Maybe that's what makes a home?)

England. What can I say about England. A twist of fate, the hand of destiny or the guiding of a higher power has led me here to this godforsaken land. Which true Irishman can call England home? There are a few redeeming features but this is no home. I remain a sojourner within this kingdom.

Let us ponder then the land of the free and the home of the brave. In all my travels, I found but one place that I felt 'at home' in all of America. A convertible, a swimming pool and a burger stand near by made this one home homely. However, I hesitate to align myself with a country that is responsible for the dual travesties of The Young And The Restless AND Woman Of My Life.

♠◇♣♡

To South Africa then. Honestly, do they put something in the water? Everyone is either tall, beautiful or both. To compound matters, there seems to be a scarcity of potatoes which merely depresses morale. No, I refuse to call a land home where they eat so much meat.

Finally comes Uganda. The land where I feel most at home yet have spent the least time. But I am destined to forever stick out like the proverbial sore thumb. I am, after all, a white man in the midst of a sea of dark faces. But these are my people. More people know my name in Gaba than in Lisburn or Northallerton or New Orleans or Simonstown. My home is on a dirt road that doesn't have a name – not on Killowen Grange, Pembury Mews, on Virgil Boulevard or St. George's Street. Yet I am reminded constantly that I'm something of a misfit in Gaba because I'm white. But it's nice when Nakyanzi tells me I'm not a *proper* white man.

14.9.05
Brompton On Swale, England

♠◇♣♡

Just My Boots

By Mark McKnight

I was followed today. Going through the taxi park, I could feel there was something wrong. I just knew there was someone behind me. So I glanced in a few taxi mirrors, took a few wrong turns, doubled back on myself but this small, shifty looking man was still following me. When I stopped to ask someone for directions (even though I didn't need to), he stopped and pretended to be talking to a taxi driver. When I sped up, he sped up too. He was on my tail for a good five minutes – a pickpocket. They rarely work alone so I had to be careful. To confront him would be a mistake. His friend would be the 'sleeper,' blending into the crowd in case things got nasty. There had been reports of all kinds of things from sleepers – throwing acid, slashing with razor blades. Some had even fired shots. It is a miracle that nobody has been killed yet.

As a rule, the white man does not mix with the general populace – he lives in his ivory tower, drives his own car and rarely enters the city. Often, he will have house staff to run his errands for him. So it is a rare occasion to see a white man in this part of the taxi park. The taxis over here only go to the slums where few white men dare to tread. I'm white so that means I'm most likely an American (I'm not going to stop to explain my Irishness to the pickpocket) which means my wallet must be fat with American dollars. I am, in every sense of the word, rich pickings to a pickpocket.

What he doesn't realise is that I have money worries of my own. In fact, I have enough money in my pocket to get the taxi almost all the way home but not quite. Depending on the benevolence of the conductor, I may have to get out before my stop and walk the rest of the way. Luckily most of the conductors along this route know me.

I can see the pickpocket is getting ready to make his move. He's getting a little bolder – he thinks I haven't noticed him. But I'm

♠◇♣♡

not the only one watching him. Just as he's about to relieve me of my wallet, there are sirens and policemen everywhere. They are screaming, 'GET DOWN ON THE GROUND!' Everybody, including the pickpocket is on the ground.

The sleeper panics, drops a long knife on the ground and makes a break for it. In this country, he should have used the knife on himself – the police take a dim view of theft and if the police don't get you, better pray that the mob doesn't either. Most likely you'll be stripped naked and chased through the streets and that's just for starters.

I could have been killed – he had a huge blade! But these are desperate people. They don't really want me dead. They just want my boots.

12.11.05
Brompton, England

Hoagies and Stoagies

By Mark McKnight

This is my damn body and I'll do what I like with it! I've been saying that ever since I can't remember. Diets? You must be joking! I will eat what I like, when I like. All that keep fit nonsense – that might be all right for you but I'm having none of it.

And I'll smoke if I want to. What's so bad about having the odd stoagy. It's not like I make a habit of it. Oh sure, I know – I've read all the information. Smoking is going to kill me, isn't it? One cigarette will take seven and a half minutes off my life I'm told. It takes me seven and a half minutes to smoke the damn thing. Does that mean I lose and extra seven and a half or when is it counted from?

And I really like to have a drink, too. What's so bad about a glass of wine with my meal? Or a pint out with my friends? It's a social thing. I wouldn't expect you to understand, of course – you're not from where I'm from. It's different here.

Problem is, my body isn't quite what it used to be. In the heady days of my youth, I was ready to conquer the world. I was strong and I was ready to take on whatever life threw at me. My body was strong too – it could take the abuse that I put it through.

Now that I'm older, though, my body doesn't seem to be able to take what it used to. I remember when we used to stay up all night and then go to work the next day. I remember when we used to eat nothing but hamburgers for days in a row. I remember drinking every night, and sometimes all day too.

These days, I wake in the morning and need a little something in the morning to get me going. The cold weather is making these old joints ache. I read the labels in the supermarket now to see how much fat is contained within.

♠◇♣♡

Forget it. My body was strong. It still is. The hoagies I have for my lunch are too damn good to give up. I won't see the doctor about these pains in my stomach – they will go away. Let me leave it another month. I know that occasionally it's hard to draw breath but everyone is like that sometimes, right? They are just like the growing pains I had when I was little. Besides, I enjoy the odd cigar. And the couple of glasses of wine that I drink when I come in from work every night won't do me any harm either.

So I am getting political. I am forming the Hoagies and Stoagies Party. Our policies are as follows:
- All diets are to be abolished
- Start a new campaign: Cigarettes and alcohol are not the devil
- You need to stop whining and mind your own business. Yes, you!

1.11.05
Brompton, England

♠◇♣♡

Of All The Girls I've Loved And Lost

By Mark McKnight

Of all the girls I've loved and lost, there is but one who even yet the pain remains buried deep within my heart.   Four   summers gone since our romance fell down beside the wayside, a victim of circumstance, or weak minds, or weak hearts, or the fragility of a perfect love.

A flaxen haired beauty from an emerald isle, we whiled away the days together.   Inhabiting our own personal oasis of calm amidst the cruel world, impenetrable and unspeakable to all but ourselves, we were enough for each other.   In the spring, our lives entwined, friendship blossomed like the apple tree outside her bedroom window.

With a name that was and ever will be sweet music to my ears, this princess gave unspoken devotion and asked for nothing in return save a warm embrace and occasionally a shoulder on which to cry. Never did I witness an angry countenance on that sweet face or hear an unkind word from those rose red lips, although for my part I plead no such innocence.   Seldom ever did I see those crystal eyes downcast: if the light that shone from those eyes might cease, the world should be the worse for it.

The rest of the world matters little when one gazes upon such a vision of loveliness but there comes a time when the devices of this world must necessarily prevail upon us.   Each day we grew closer over Irish steak, Italian ice cream, Chilean red wine and good old Dixieland jazz.   Thus my final memory of this whole passionate affair remains as a silver haired and silver tongued pianist who couldn't or wouldn't play 'Fly Me To The Moon' by Frank Sinatra.   Without her song, a perfect evening ended and we parted ways.

With passage booked on the next boat leaving Belfast, I could do nothing but watch her go.   Nothing so clichéd as walking into the sunset; rather the only woman I have ever truly loved embraced me, bid

♠◇♣♡

her fond farewell and entered the townhouse that for so long had been the fixation of my fantasies of love.

For my own part, I boarded a steamer bound for distant and exotic lands on a cold, foggy Belfast morning. During those halcyon days after my departure we communicated frequently: letters sent by airmail across the wide oceans of the world and an occasional telegram. I visited places the like of which I had only dreamed, from the dry Sahara to the blue glaciers of the Arctic, ever a sojourner in foreign domains.

A mere Summer, Autumn and Winter did I roam, eight months apart from friends, family and my first love. But my return lacked all of the warmth and tenderness I had known of yesteryear. The fire of our passion no longer smouldered, our romance fallen down beside the wayside, a victim of circumstance, or weak minds, or weak hearts, or the fragility of a perfect love. Of all the girls I've loved and lost, there is but one...

17.8.05
Gaba, Uganda

♠◇♣♡

First Day Of The Rest Of Our Lies

By Mark McKnight

I remember our marriage ceremony as if it was yesterday. We stood at the front of a packed church and declared our undying love to each other. To have and to hold, in sickness and in health, for richer for poorer. It was a beautiful night. That night, as we sat on a Mediterranean beach, we made some more promises to each other. The one I remember the most clearly was the promise that we would never, ever lie to one another. And I meant it – I really did, but the idealistic promises of two star-crossed lovers often mean little in the real world.

For the entire honeymoon, I can put my hand on my heart and say that I never did lie to my wife. For a three week honeymoon, that's quite a feat. Not one single little white lie to put a black mark on my clean conscience.

The problem came when we returned home to the real world after the honeymoon was over. Back to the bleak November rain in the north of England, it soon became clear that we did not know everything about one another, or at least we had not discussed it together.

Both from important underworld families, research had been carried out by a more criminal form of a private eye so that we both knew what we were getting into. I knew who she was and she knew that I knew that she knew. She knew who I was and I knew that she knew. Confused?

But information had been wrong in the past: the so-called 'missing' – individuals who had recklessly admitted their familial links to the wrong person. So when, on the way back from the airport we were discussing what we liked to do with our spare time, neither of us was willing to be the first to admit that we were involved with the British equivalent of La Cosa Nostra.

As something of a chord basher on my uncle's old acoustic guitar, I told her all about my guitar playing, that I really wanted to

♠◇♣♡

play in a band. She told me about her badminton club that she belonged to, that she wanted to play in a team. We were both clearly lying. We both knew that the other was lying. We both knew that the other knew that we were lying. But just like with all lies, the lie took on a mind of its own. I had to talk my way out of the lie to iron out the inconsistencies. I had to buy a guitar the next day to make it look like I hadn't been lying. She joined a badminton club the next day and bought a badminton racket.

For now, though, as we drove home from the airport, we both knew that the other had not told the whole truth but we were either unwilling or unable to confront the other. After all, this was the first day of the rest of our lies.

12.11.05
Brompton, England

♠◇♣♡

The Death Card
By Mark McKnight

This is the only place in the world where the best musicians aren't the ones on stage in the clubs but rather playing on the street. There are only two places to hear real Dixie in Dixie: Preservation Hall and St. Louis' Square.

Preservation Hall has a sign on the wall: Requests - $5. Saints - $10. The old band leader slowly makes his way to the stage, pulls a battered trumpet from its case and puts it to his lips but as he begins to play, the years fall away. He is old and grey but his playing is effortless: old men preserving their old music in this Preservation Hall. There's no bar, no food and no proper seats to speak of – just a few rickety old wooden benches. Preservation Hall is the bastion of the old guard of jazz.

On the streets around St. Louis cathedral is the new guard of an old, old music. For the jazz band on the street is full of vibrancy and youthful vigour. Doreen is the clarinet player and band leader – a rotund, jocund black lady who represents the heart and soul of this city. She's been knocked down more times than she can count but she pours her heart and soul into her clarinet every day on the streets of New Orleans. In all my travels, I have never seen a musician with as much soul as Doreen. She's like a clarinet playing version of Aretha.

This band isn't employed by the city. They play here every day because they love the music. They are buskers in the truest sense of the word. When they play, it doesn't take long for a crowd to gather. At the end of every set, they pass the hat and good naturedly hassle passers by for their money and spare change. They shout, "Applause is nice, but it don't pay for no red beans and rice!"

Around St. Louis Square sit the gypsy fortune tellers. On a whim, my fortune is told by an amiable looking tarot reader who had adorned his table with feathers and crystals. The cards are shuffled and

♠◇♣♡

I am instructed to choose one card. The death card. I look aghast at my choice. The fortune teller offers precious little comfortable counsel for we both understand the significance of my choice.

The icy fingers of fate or a higher power have brushed the cheek of this city. Two days later, Hurricane Katrina hits the Louisiana coast. Submerged beneath about eight feet of water, the Vieux Carre now lives only in the memories of those who created the music and those who listened. The death card drawn on that mild September morning was not for me but for an entire city. Yet the spirit of a city cannot die. Occasionally, one imagines hearing Doreen's clarinet singing around what was St. Louis Square, from flooded doorways and empty buildings. One day, jazz will once again be heard on the streets of New Orleans.

7.11.05
Brompton, England

♠◇♣♡

Ice Cool

By Mark McKnight

When I was a kid, the only thing cooler than being cool was being ice cool. And everybody wanted to be ice cool. Being ice cool was more important than school. In fact, if you were too cool for school, you were proper cool. Being ice cool was more important than girls, more important than football, more important than sweets and way more important than your mum and dad and teacher.

There was a much discussed code if you wanted to be cool – the Rules of Cool! If you dressed right, walked right, talked right, listened to the right music, ate the right food, rode the right bike, had the right lunch box, wore the right clothes, liked the right things and watched the right TV programmes, then you might be, just maybe, ice cool.

All my life (well, the first seventeen years or so of it), I wanted nothing more than to be ice cool. And I tried – I really tried so hard. But you know, I was never going to make the grade. For a start, I wore glasses from age seven. Next, I didn't have the right hair cut. If your mum cut your hair, you were not cool. I didn't have the right bike – when you needed a BMX to be cool, I had a chopper. When I got a BMX instead, you needed a chopper to be cool. I had a dimpled chin, or I didn't have a dimpled chin. My ears were too big or they were too small. I had too much hair on my chest or I didn't have enough. My feet were too big or too small. I was too good at sport or I was too good at music or I wasn't good enough at maths or I liked art or I didn't like geography or I played the saxophone or I didn't play the piano.

Because no matter how hard I tried to be cool, I never quite made the cut. Forget ice cool. I didn't even make it into the cool category. However, I did have a nemesis. Paul Rhodes. Even now, I feel the venom on my lips as I say his name. For Paul Rhodes was,

♠◇♣♡

according to contemporary popular opinion, the epitome of 'ice cool.' You couldn't help but love him. And he had a girlfriend too.

Then one night when I was seventeen, I woke up in a cold sweat. I realised that being ice cool is nothing to do with Paul Rhodes. It's got nowt to do with the clothes you wear or the music you listen to. I began to comprehend the futility of my efforts. For my friends are not the ones who define ice cool. I am. If I think I'm ice cool, then I am.

I haven't reached that stage yet and I hope I am never that conceited but I've realised that I'm a lot cooler than I used to think I was.

'I'm as cold as ice...'

2.11.05
Brompton, England

♠◇♣♡

Killaloe

By Mark McKnight

When I signed up, it was for the money, pure and simple. A few hundred quid a month for playing my saxophone was too good to pass up. Steady work and since it was for queen and country, the money was guaranteed to arrive without having to negotiate with a reluctant boss – the queen looks after her own. So by the time my security clearance came through to play as a bandsman with the North Irish Territorial Army Band, I was laughing all the way to the bank.

As reservists, we were meant to rehearse a full day and a half every week but since we were all professional musicians, we usually did about half of that. But we still got paid for a full six days per month. And that didn't include gigs. They used to say that we were one of the best bands in the British army with some of the worst military skills.

Our regimental march was Killaloe – the one song that we were guaranteed to play at every gig. I don't think there was even any music for it – it just got handed down from the old boys to the new recruits like me. I especially loved the cheer at the end. No other regiment's march was quite like ours.

But what the bandmaster failed to mention when he recruited most of us was that we might actually be called upon to die for our country. Oh sure, it was fun while I was playing my saxophone in Ireland at pass off parades and dinner nights. Then our commander in chief decided to invade another oil rich country. The conflict escalated and soon they were calling up reservists. Like our unit.

With next to no skills, our band was sent to war. In war, old men talk and young men die. This war was no exception. Our band was attached to 152 Ambulance Regiment so we were affectionately known as 'humpers and dumpers.' No medical skills so our only real use was as stretcher bearers and some of us as drivers. Daily, we saw

♠◇♣♡

the spoils of war – young soldiers cut down in their prime for a cause of which they knew or cared little.

As reservists, we were kept away from the front lines – our field hospital was well away from the thick of the battle. Two weeks before our tour of duty was due to come to an end, our camp was hit by a missile from one of our 'allies.' What is euphemistically regarded as friendly fire rained down on what was our home for the last six months.

Most of the unit was wiped out but for some reason I survived. We should have gone home tomorrow. Death is coming. I can feel it. Gangrene has set in to one of my legs and the other has already been amputated. I won't last much longer. I have only one dying wish – whatever happens, ask them to play Killaloe at my funeral.

10.10.05
Brompton On Swale, England

Forever Autumn

By Mark McKnight

Why, oh why did I ever have to open my big mouth? I had never had things so good and then I went and ruined everything.

It all started about two years ago. I never went to school and without an education, the only jobs around here are those for house boys. If you're lucky, you'll get a good master who takes care of you. Those who aren't so lucky get beaten almost every day. But who can we complain to? We are the forgotten ones – the untouchable caste of this society.

Luckily, my master was a good one. He only beat me occasionally and I usually deserved it. So I worked hard for this master but times were hard and eventually he had to let me go – he just couldn't afford to keep me on any longer. He promised that I could stay until he had found me a new job. About two weeks later, my master came home beaming – he had found me a new job with a new master.

The new master was strict but fair. If I worked hard for him, my job was safe. If I was ever found to be sleeping on the job or stealing then I would be on the street immediately. Other offences would be dealt with severely but would not result in my dismissal. This seemed like a fair deal.

The bane of my existence was a tree in the middle of my master's compound. This tree shed leaves throughout the year. Through four seasons this tree would drop leaves to taunt me. The world around might be Spring – the newborn lambs in the fields and the flowers coming into bloom but this tree was forever Autumn.

As the houseboy, it was my job to keep the compound neat and tidy. Every morning I would rise early to sweep the compound which really meant sweep the leaves from this most quarrelsome of trees. I even tried to take action to prevent this tree from shedding its foliage – I ploughed manure from the goats into the soil around the roots and removed any other plants that might be stealing nutrients. It seemed that nothing would stop this tree giving up its purple leaves.

I talked the matter over with the master's son – it seemed silly to sweep the leaves every day from this one tree. Why not cut the tree down and replace it with a hardier sapling that would not discard so easily?

And so my master's son set to work with an axe that I had sharpened especially for the job. With a few swift blows, the tree was no more. The blight on my otherwise happy life was gone.

Early the following morning, I rose to clean the compound. With the tree gone, I could not give the impression of work because there was simply no work to do. My master watched me for a time and then my job was lost – a victim to my own stupidity.

29.10.05
Brompton, England

♠◇♣♡

Sex By The Shilling

By Mark McKnight

When we checked in to the Hotel Charmi, we didn't quite realise what sort of a joint it was – in all innocence, we really did expect it to be a normal hotel. The price we were quoted seemed somewhat low: 1,500/= (shillings) per night for a room. That's less than a dollar.

So we stashed our luggage and went in search of food. The hotel bar was serving food so we didn't need to venture too far. We sat at a table on the sidewalk long into the night, watching, waiting, talking and generally enjoying one another's company.

It was long after dark when we retired and it quickly became apparent why the rooms were so cheap – the hotel made most of its money from 'additional services' in the form of young ladies who were clearly drugged to the eyeballs and offering all manner of sordid and sleazy services which, by the noise, our neighbour was currently availing himself of.

How much? Baby, if I was going to sell my body, I would hope to be making a lot more than that. I always thought that if I ever had to pay for sex I'd pay more than that – it just seems awfully cheap. You're worth more than that. No thanks, it's not my scene but good luck!

When we arose and checked out the next morning, we were charged not 1,500/= but 15,000/= for the room. It was only in retrospect that we realised why – since we had not availed ourselves of any of the hotel's 'additional services,' the hotel did not make any money off us so they put the price of the room up.

The two white men arrived early in the evening. All the girls saw them and suddenly the tension rose in the hotel – white men's

♠♢♣♡

money was always good but they were few and far between. But why had they stopped in Masaka? Few people stop in Masaka on purpose and hardly any of them are white. Most of the town remains destroyed after a civil war that ended twenty years ago. It is nothing but a stopping point for fuel on the way through to somewhere else: Rwanda or the Congo.

As they sit at a table on the sidewalk, eating, drinking, laughing and telling stories, some of the girls give up and go to service their regulars. Others hit the streets to try to stimulate some business (no pun intended).

Eventually they leave their table and I just happen to be the only girl left in the courtyard. At fifteen, men seem to want me so I try to strike up a conversation. In broken English, I tell them my price. In flawless Luganda, one tells me that I'm worth more. But they don't want any action tonight. They look like aid workers – probably don't have much money anyway. As they leave, I begin to weep. For the first time in my life, someone has told me that I am worth something.

29.10.05
Brompton, England

♠◇♣♡

Samurai Fast Food

By Mark McKnight

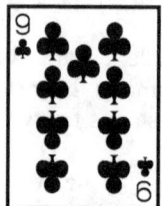

Despite the horrific cliché, it is true. I am a samurai warrior and I now run a sushi restaurant. With my blade skills, it seemed an obvious career move. Of course, I miss the good old days. I was known as the Green Dragon – a name that was never spoken, only whispered reverentially.

Young samurais were weaned on legends of my crusades. With each telling, the legends grew, for none had seen the face of the Green Dragon, at least not knowingly. Every samurai knew of the blade I carried. Made entirely of black oak with the motif of lilies carved into the hilt, it was said that even with the blunt edge of a wooden sword, I could cut a man in half.

Many challengers had come and failed to defeat the Green Dragon. And with every victory, the stories grew, for I did not kill my defeated challengers. Rather, I left them to tell of their near death experiences at the hands of the greatest samurai the world has ever seen. I branded them on the back of their left hand that all would know of their defeat by the Green Dragon.

I have heard all kinds of tales told of the Green Dragon. Apparently I could disappear at will. There was even a story went about that I could not be killed by a normal sword. The only way to defeat me was with a wooden blade, like my own but made of the white ash tree –yin to the yang of my own black oak weapon.

The legend goes that the only man ever to defeat me went by the name of Tom Salvador, a name that is even now, years later, etched on my mind. Many years have passed since our dawn battle began on a lonely African hillside. The man they call the Messiah had given him the white ash sword that he fought with. For three long hours the mêlée raged with neither warrior able to gain the upper hand. Finally, a foe worthy of the fray was here.

♠◊♣♡

As the sun reached its zenith, Salvador found reserves of strength where I had none. We had somehow exchanged swords during the combat. As Salvador stood over me and called for his own sword, the white ash blade that would deliver my death blow, the wind began to whisper in the trees. As Salvador dropped his blade, I had vanished – defeated by an unkempt American with no honour.

So now I prepare sushi, certain that one day in the not too distant future, Salvador will enter my restaurant and I must once again commence battle with this worthy adversary. Yet I am handicapped. Without my blade I am naked – the black oak sword that Tom Salvador has kept since I disappeared on that dewy African mid-morning. When he returns I shall be ready. For in this country, the red oak grows. I shall have a new blade and warriors will fear me once more.

29.10.05
Brompton, England

♠◊♣♡

Melanie

By Mark McKnight

Her name was Melanie and we were in love. The first and last on my list of 'girls who I have really, really, really loved.' Admittedly, I was just a youngster of six years old but the fickle hand of love cares little for age, race, creed or social status. Like the eternal story of Romeo and Juliet, our love was perfect all those years ago.

Those who write pop songs about love, the modern day Shakespeares speak of the trappings of a perfect life: a man has his house, his car, his friends and most of all his woman. I too had the trappings of my perfect life: my bike, my Optimus Prime transformer, my best friend Ryan and most of all I had my woman. Or my girl at least.

Quite the ladies' man, I seem to recall it had taken me some time to settle on Melanie as my girl. I fear my talents have diminished somewhat since those heady days of youth – all that remains is to reminisce on a long forgotten childhood.

I was John Travolta to her Olivia Newton John. With a stunning blonde at my side, I was the envy of the school. At any rate, I was the envy of my best friend Ryan which, to a six year old, is all that really matters.

As the honeymoon period of our relationship came and went, we began to have what the euphemist calls 'lover's tiffs.' Looking back, there were mistakes on both sides.

Like every member of our male species, I lacked the emotional intelligence to properly express my feelings. Remember when you were six and the only way you could show a girl that you like her was by pulling her hair or pinching her? I had no words to express the heartfelt devotion that was burning up inside of me so I pulled her hair and pinched her on the playground. An error which, to my discredit, I may not yet have learned my lesson.

♠◇♣♡

I do not hold myself entirely responsible for this breakdown in
our relationship. She was quite simply insatiable. Every playtime she
would demand that we play 'Catch and Kiss,' a game of which the
rules are self-explanatory from the title – when you catch someone, you
get to kiss them. I fear she misunderstood the desires of the six year
old on the inside of every grown man: to play transformers and wrestle
with his friends.

But the cataclysm for our affair came when parents got
involved – as a six year old, I held few bargaining chips during the
protracted negotiations over this complicated match. At any rate, it
spelled the end for our tryst. Neither side was willing to reach a
compromise to make the match work. Without a dowry, we were
powerless to perpetuate this ill fated liaison.

I can conclude no better than the simple inscription inside the
back cover of my ragged P3 maths exercise book: Mark loves Melanie,
dated April 1985.

5.9.05
Brompton On Swale, England

♠◇♣♡

Movie Star

By Mark McKnight

In my life, I have been accidentally many things – accidentally in love, accidentally here, accidentally there. But the worst accident of all was the day I became accidentally famous.

I never wanted fame and fortune. Certainly the trappings of success (money, nice house, fancy car) had their attractions but I only ever wanted for a simple life. So it came as quite a shock to me when the movie studio approached me to make my life into a movie.

If truth be told, my life is not worthy of a motion picture – I just did what any other man would have done, given the same circumstances. For I am a survivor. I have been to the brink of death four times now with a brain tumour. A cancer, eating me up from the inside out. All I did was to keep fighting – never to give up, never to lose hope that my time on this rolling sphere was not yet at an end.

Four times my skull has been opened up and a team of doctors has poked and prodded, cut and sewn the sinews and tissues inside my cranium. Four times I have once again been sealed. Four times I have watched doctors shake their heads, sigh a little and then tell me they have done all they can. Four times they have told me I might never walk again. Four times I have astounded all the medical evidence and clawed my way back from oblivion.

And so they want to make me into a movie. I am Kevin Costner or he is me. They ask my advice, they listen when I tell them my story. On set, I tell them it didn't happen that way, but it happened like this…

Day after day we shoot. Some days I am up to it, some days I am not. Some days I can't even get out of bed. When the movie is finished, I wait for the premiere – I don't want to see any advance screenings. By now, I am a household name – the media machine has

♠◇♣♡

endlessly recycled my story in hype before the movie release. Serialisations. Chat show appearances.

I walk slowly along the red carpet into the theatre. The carrion press ask for photos and sound bytes. My minders shepherd me to my seat.

Now I am a movie star of sorts. The world has seen my picture a thousand times. The man with half a brain – the other half a victim to the tumours, carefully excised by skilled hands.

I have arrived. Yet as the final credits roll, I feel a familiar throbbing inside my head. A throbbing that turned out to be the first tumour. I can feel it growing again. If they remove any more of my brain, it may kill me. If they don't, I may die anyway. I fear this immortalisation on celluloid is the converse of the passing of my mortal life on this planet.

Farewell from an accidental movie star.

3.11.05
Brompton, England

Football, Football, Football

By Mark McKnight

Football, football, football. That's all we ever hear in this house. Me dad and me support the local team and I'm going to play for them some day. Me mam doesn't understand. She doesn't see why the two men in her life have to disappear every Saturday afternoon to watch 'a bunch of grown men chase after a bag of air.' She doesn't understand. But me and me dad know – football IS life.

On the pitch, nothing else matters but your team – getting the ball up front and scoring goals. So every afternoon on the way home from school, me dad and me stop at the park and kick the ball around for a while. He tells me what goalkeepers do. He tells me what the strikers do. I think I want to be a winger. I'm fast so he thinks I'll be dead good.

Some of the men in the stands sing songs with words in them that me dad tells me he doesn't want to ever hear me saying but sometimes when I'm playing with me mates I sing the songs. I get in trouble off me teachers but I don't care – if you support a team, you have to sing the songs.

I know all the player's names – where they play, what they're good at, what they aren't. I know how to shout at the referee. I know where we are in the league. Me and me dad have season tickets so that means we get to come and see every game. How mint is that? Sometimes we don't go to the away games though – me dad says it's too far to drive.

Me dad is the best. He knows everything there is to know about football. He used to play for the Harriers when he was young. He even used to get paid. He was professional footballer you know.

I just can't believe it – a heart attack. Me dad died of a heart attack. We were holding hands and singing in the stand and he just fell

♠◇♣♡

down dead, right there in the Adam W. Slean Memorial stand. I thought he was joking but they had to get the ambulance and everything. I dunno – its just like I feel when I get a red card – just like crap. How could me dad have a heart attack? He's so strong. Like Fergusson who plays up front for the Saints. Just like a super hero. You know, me dad knows everything there is to know about football. Oh. I mean 'knew.' He knew everything there is to know about football.

There's just me and mam now – I'm the man of the house. What am I going to do? Mam doesn't even know how to play football. Who's going to take me to watch the home games now? Who's going to kick a ball with me in the park? I'll never be able to play for the Saints if I don't have somebody to practise with me.

Dad?

DAAAAAAAAAAD!!!

1.11.05
Brompton, England

Urlay Nook

By Mark McKnight

Urlay Nook is a very odd place. I suppose you could say it's just like any other village, here where the moors sweep downwards towards the sea. The problem with Urlay Nook, so far as I see it, is that it doesn't exist.

Last afternoon as I idled my carriage along the king's highway, I chanced upon a signpost directing me towards Urlay Nook. As my friend, Albert Knot, hails from Urlay Nook, I thought it only prudent that I should drop by to call in on his humble abode.

So I tugged the left rein, signalling to Robert (my pony) my intent to sample the fayre that Urlay Nook had to offer and dutifully, Robert (my pony) carried me and the trap along the road to Urlay Nook.

All was well or so I thought as the sun beat down on our well travelled backs but it wasn't long before the problem with Urlay Nook became more and more apparent. Passing through Long Newton, Apple Green and, of course, both Greater and Lesser Frogbottom, Robert (my pony) turned his head with a look as if to say, 'This Urlay Nook which you seek, I fear it is not...'

Blessed with uncanny insight and wisdom for a pony, I immediately knew that Robert (my pony) had, so to speak, hit the nail on the head. Of course, the pedant will assume that Robert (my pony) had not yet finished his sentence. I can merely reply by saying he may have finished, or maybe not. But it is not if we finish or not, rather whether we meant it or not. And clearly, Robert (my pony) did not mean it, otherwise he would not have said 'not.' One thing is, however, absolutely certain; Robert (my pony) and I were not going to find Urlay Nook this day because quite simply, it was not.

Being the pensive type, I began to consider the philosophical consequences of this new development. If Urlay Nook was 'not,' could

♠◇♣♡

there be other places that were similarly 'not.' It was then that a most worrying thought occurred to Robert (my pony). If the village of Urlay Nook was 'not,' what proof could there possible be that Robert (my pony) himself was also 'not.' That would certainly create a problem with the ongoing locomotion of my trap if Robert (my pony) was 'not' as I travelled towards (or possible away from) the village of Urlay Nook that we now know is 'not.'

But the greatest scandal is yet to come for, if both the village of Urlay Nook and Robert (my pony) are both 'not,' then it is quite possible that my friend Albert Knot is also 'not.' As Robert (my pony) and I continued in our journey, we came upon another signpost. As luck would have it, we had simply taken a wrong turn. How happy we were when we discovered that Urlay Nook, Robert (my pony) and Albert Know were all in fact not 'not!'

31.8.05
Brompton On Swale, England

113

♠◇♣♡

Living Next Door To Nigel

By Mark McKnight

Nigel is this guy who lived next door. I don't know how it started – to begin with it was a bit of fun but everything just fell apart. You see, the walls between our terraced houses were paper thin. When he was watching movies late at night, I could listen in surround sound. When my girlfriend came over, Nigel listened in on our afternoon snogging. But she's gone now and it's mostly Nigel's fault. Nigel and I used to go to the pub of an evening for a couple of jars but as time went by, we started going to the pub more and more and I started going to work less and less. That's the thing about working for such an enormous company. Nobody really cares when you don't show up for work. I don't even know if Nigel had a job.

But when Caitlin found out that I was going to the pub instead of work, she hit the roof. I mean, it was pretty bad for her – who wants a lazy, alcoholic, skiver boyfriend? A nice, professional girl like her doesn't date a piss artist like me. I'm not excusing my behavior. I know I was a shit. But that's no excuse for what she did. Not that there was any bunny boiling or anything, but I guess I deserved everything I got. Yes sir, I was the Sultan of Shits.

I didn't think Nigel would kick me in the balls like that though. I was a shit, he was the Prince of Bastards. Oh, he was smooth – I'll give him that. He took advantage of a vulnerable young woman who had just split with her shit of a boyfriend. His silver tongue lured her right into his bed and I was able to listen in Dolby Digital 5.1 Stereo Surround sound through the paper thin wall between Nigel's bedroom and my own. They really loved rubbing my nose in it. Four times! All night long like bloody rabbits.

What could I do? What would any sane man do? Not even Arthur Guinness' ole' black magic was able to numb the pain this time. I was justified in my actions – these were extenuating circumstances.

♠◇♣♡

That probably won't hold up in a court of law though. The legal profession has a very narrow minded concept of right and wrong. Long live Post-Modernism – that's what I say. There's no such thing as absolute right and wrong! Well, this sure feels right for me. I was justified in my actions considering the circumstances, wasn't I? I suppose it's too late for introspection now.

The bastard! The bitch! But all is fair in love and war: the yin and the yang are once again in balance. Equilibrium has been restored to the lower middle class – I got what I deserved and I gave them exactly what they deserved. I don't know where things go from here but I suppose I won't be hearing Nigel through the paper thin walls any more.

23.10.04
Durham, England

Fat Bottomed Girl

By Mark McKnight

WOW!!!! Will you just look at that? That is one SERIOUS ass. I mean in a competition of butts, that would be the hands down winner. I wonder does she have to book two seats on the plane to fit in? There's no way she could fit into one seat. That is a girl who has serious weight problems. As they say, it's probably hormonal. Yeah right – hormones from cream cakes! Still, I shouldn't make jokes about people being fat.

Oh no, she's coming over to talk to me. Quick, look for an escape. Oh no, too slow. She's spotted me. Please don't come to me, please don't come to me.

"Hi, my name is Emma…" and so we're off and talking. I can already see the snickering in the background from my mates. It reminds me of a joke about mopeds and fat girls but it's too rude to put in print. Suffice to say, the punchline involves the phrase, 'until your mates find out.' There's no hiding from it – my mates are watching me being chatted up by this fat chick. I'll never live it down.

But as I talk to Emma, she turns out to be a really sweet girl. I'm not on the pull tonight so we stand at the bar chatting as my mates one by one succumb to the beer goggles and pull girls that have to put it bluntly, fallen out of the ugly tree, hit every branch on the way down, landed in the ugly fire and then been beaten out by the ugly shovel. Emma could at least lose weight. If you're ugly, you're ugly.

To my surprise, I discover that Emma has a personality and a wonderful one at that. As time wears on, I find that I am becoming more and more attracted to Emma. She's funny, she's interested in me and most of all, she couldn't give a flying fig what other people think of her. I don't think she even knows that she's fat.

All too soon, kicking out time comes around so we hastily swap numbers and promise to talk soon. This hurried exchange is

♠◇♣♡

necessary in this particular nightclub – well known for the fights in the car park at closing time. Neither of us wants to miss a ringside seat at this weekly ritual so we go our separate ways and join the crowds outside who are waiting for this week's brawls to begin.

Next day, I decide to phone Emma – her number written on an old receipt in my wallet. There is no answer and I leave a message on her voicemail.

But the story has a sting in its tail for as I drive home from work, I hear my message on a local radio station – I am a victim of a practical joke. I have bared my soul on the most popular radio station in the region. Forget chatting to a fat bird. Now I'll <u>never</u> live it down with my mates.

1.11.05
Brompton, England

Pimps And Pool Cues

By Mark McKnight

I'm just hanging out in the bar where we go on a Friday and Saturday evening. Despite the Guinness being rank in this part of the world, I'm persevering. A bottle of that old black magic adds weight and substance to one's claim of true Irish heritage here, particularly for people like me who don't really have a true Irish heritage. So we're playing pool, the same way we do every Friday and Saturday evening. Not looking to score, or pick up chicks or whatever way you want to put it.

There's this girl at the other side of the bar room giving me the eye. I've seen her a couple of time checking me out. She doesn't waste any time either. During a brief lull in the incessant 'cheese' coming from the DJ, she asks if I want to 'hang out.' She's a pretty girl but my name is next on the chalkboard to play the next game of pool. So I make an excuse and she returns to her spot over at the bar.

This brief moment gives me a chance to rethink my position. In this town, there is only one reason why a pretty young girl would be drinking at a bar by herself. What a shame she's on the game – she seems like an intelligent young lady. Things could go either way. Turning her down may be the biggest mistake I'll ever make. Her pimp won't be too far away and they sometimes don't take too kindly to white men who aren't interested.

My real Irish friend has seen what's going on too and has already spotted the pimp. Concealed in a booth with his muscle, he already looks miserable. You'd think that he would be a bit happier with the money he must be making. In this part of town, there are no two bit whores – you have to pay top dollar for these girls. Not like the ones who approach you on the street. Irish pretends he can't talk when this happens – it's funny to watch them try to communicate.

♠◇♣♡

With a nod from the pimp, the girl makes another pass. Her opening gambit is a traditional one – do I have a light for her cigarette but she once again retires to the bar when she realises that her progress is at best limited.

With a nod from Irish, I realise it's time to leave. I didn't think it possible but the pimp looks more miserable. Angry too. So we abandon our game and get out of the bar fast. Maybe we can get some fried chicken or something.

Somehow, the muscle make it to the street before us. They hold us from behind. The pimp is in front. A knife. Irish lunges head first. A sickening thud. A broken nose. Blood everywhere. Confusion. We twist free. Irish has the knife. A struggle. Hands grabbing. More blood. Running. Screaming.

Women and Guinness! Always a dangerous combination, no matter how Irish you really are.

31.10.05
Brompton, England